Lies and Luck

Twenty short stories

NOEL SPENCE

An Oswica Publication

First published in 2004
ISBN 0 9548251 1 X
Printed by Universities Press Ltd.

For Heather...

CONTENTS

THE GIFT

The young man's anger dissolved with the girl's first tear. In an instant his arm was round her shoulder and he was comforting her, patting her hair, kissing away her tears. How many times down the centuries, I wondered, in how many continents and cultures, had that little scene been enacted.

I was on one of the public seats in Eyre Square, the centre of Galway, the most western city of the European Union. Yes, a city on the outer edge of the Economic Community, but seeming to me, in its easygoing cosmopolitan assurance, to represent the European ideal much more comfortably than many of the bigger continental centres I had visited.

There were only a few days left of my trip round Ireland. I had found the place irresistible. The nation wore its new-found wealth and political importance like an expensive dress that enhanced natural charm without threatening personal identity. Now, as I discreetly watched the little human drama on the next seat along, in the shadow of the famed hooker sail sculptures and to the beat of a busy commercial centre on a sunny August lunchtime, I somehow felt a pleasing sense of synthesis, of old and new, changeless and changing.

"Never judge a woman by her tears," interrupted a voice beside me. I looked round quickly. The owner of the voice was a large man, probably in his fifties, although he had one of those slightly ruddy, unlined faces that frustrate accurate age estimation. His white hair was brushed back with some style. He wore a dark gray suit that took no notice at all of the strong sun in a clear blue sky.

"Sorry?" I said, although it was clear he had been watching me watching the little episode next door.

He smiled. "Aye, you're right about that. It's sorry you'd be for sure."

"No, I meant ...I wasn't sure if it was me...what you said..."

The man smiled again. "D'you see that arm?" He sat down on the bench beside me and held the limb in question out for inspection. "And that leg? There's two pins in that arm. There's more plates and screws and pins in that leg than I can remember, and, for good measure, there's three toes missing off the foot."

By now I was confident the man wasn't playing with a full deck, so I merely nodded and said nothing. He settled himself into a comfortable position and looked round expansively.

"And how are you likin' our new image? Beggars askin' you for Euro and cents, your Irish Stew served to you by waiters from Albania? You can buy your Irish shillelagh now from B&Q, but it's been made in Poland or China." He laughed. "That's if you can find the store, mind. The last visitor askin' if there was a B&Q in Galway was told maybe, but there was definitely a G and a Y in it."

I laughed too, rapidly revising my opinion of him. "Are you a local man yourself, then? What's the word, a Galwegian?"

"Well, I am and I'm not. I'm from the Islands. I'm a Man of Aran. We're a race of our own. I married a girl from the town here, just the same, and settled out on the far side of Salthill. She was a fine girl too." The thought seemed to take him away from me, but reminded me of his original remark. I waited a few moments, and drew him back to it.

"So you can't judge a woman by her tears, you say?"

He turned to face me, the sun backlighting the long strands of hair and tinting them gold. He seemed to be studying me, as if considering my worthiness for an explanation. The reply, when it came, was oddly off target.

"To tell you the truth, sir, I'm probably more of a stranger meself in Galway now than you are, and you a visitor passin' through."

He paused to roll himself a cigarette, and I noticed a slight trembling in the left hand that held the paper. It was the arm with the pins implanted.

"I was a fisherman from the minute I was born on that island. It was a hard life but a good one. Sometimes I think I should never have left it. Well, no matter." He sucked long and hard at the thin cigarette. "When we were still young men, about 25 or 26, me and Aidan, me best mate, packed it in and started work here in the town on the buildin' sites. There was plenty of work and good money. Aidan was me Best Man when I married Barbara. They were good times."

He paused for such a long time that I thought he judged the story over, but he suddenly stubbed out his cigarette and continued it. "It'll be twenty three years next month. I was comin' home from Sligo on me bike, a 500 Yamaha. I was comin' round a corner when I met a car head-on, right on me own side of the road. I found out later he was a German tourist. He'd pulled out from a picnic area and forgot he shoulda been drivin' on the left. I remember the car right on me and thinkin' there was no hope of missin' it. That's all.

They told me later that the first Garda officer on the scene took one look at me and told the ambulance men when they arrived that I was a morgue case. I'm glad they didn't take his word for it. The first thing I remember was wakenin' up stuck all over with tubes and a man in a white coat lookin' down at me.

'Where am I?' I asked him.

'I C U.'

'I see you too,' I said, 'but where are the two of us?' It turned out I was in Intensive Care. I'd been out cold for nine days. It was ten weeks before I was allowed home, with more metal than bone in this arm and leg."

At that moment the subjects of our original exchange sauntered past hand in hand, their disagreement as forgotten as the previous day's newspapers stuffed in the litter cage beside us. The man glanced at them and gave that same little smile.

"She visited me twice a day the whole time I was in hospital. Never missed once, and her livin' away out on the other side of the town. No man could have asked for a better woman. Nor for a better mate. Aidan came to see me every chance he had. Sometimes he was able to bring Barbara or give her a lift home."

The man put away his cigarette materials, and prepared to go on his way.

"But what about the tears?" I heard myself asking, in some desperation.

He stopped. "Ah, the tears, the tears surely. They came nearly a year after the accident. I came home one day and there she was standin' at the front of the house with the tears drownin' her. I thought maybe her ma had died, or somethin' like that, but she was sobbin' that hard I couldn't find out at first what was wrong with her. I was comfortin' her all I could when she told me...

All those tears I was pityin' her for, all those tears rollin' down her face, they were every one for the man she loved, the man who had just left her for another woman, the man who had been me best friend for nearly 30 years, and Best Man at our weddin'. She and Aidan had been havin' an affair behind me back almost from the day Barbara and me got married, long before the accident happened.

I never suspected a thing all that time. Can you believe that? How did they do it? How could they keep it from me every day for all those years? She told me everything. You know the terrible thing? She didn't care what I thought or felt when she was tellin' me, all her feelin's were for Aidan, the man who had now betrayed her and me both."

"I'm sorry, I'm really sorry. It must have been a terrible shock for you. What did you do?"

He looked up with a strange little smile. "What did I do? I'll tell you what I did. I went away for a week and thought things over. Then I came back with a gallon of petrol and I burned the house to the ground, with her in it, in the marriage bed she had defiled. Then I went out to Aidan's house and blew his head away with his own shotgun. Y'see, the man you're talkin' to, sir, is what the papers at the time called 'a double murderer'. I'm just out of Limerick Jail after doin' twenty-two years. The judge said I had to do twenty-five, but I'm out with three to spare."

He paused, but I was too taken aback to form any reply. "I had drink on me that night when I done them. I took a vow in me prison cell that I'd never let the stuff touch me lips again, and I never have. That's the only good thing, sir, that has come out of the whole bad business."

The sun was beating down mercilessly. People were finishing outdoor lunches and starting to head back to offices and businesses, but as I made my way back to the hotel, a shiver was running through me, like I was coming down with a chill.

The Commodore is one of those little privately owned, personally run hotels that almost guarantee you creaking floorboards and faded red velvet curtains with gold cord tie-backs. I was sitting in the Residents' Lounge that same afternoon trying to remember a poem we had read in primary school where an old sailor tells a guest at a wedding the story of a terrible crime he had committed. He'd killed a condor or eagle or some such sacred bird. Needless to say, I was identifying with the Wedding Guest.

The hotel owner, Mr Cassidy, a little man with one extraordinary strand of hair coiled round and round his head in a doomed effort to hide a bald dome, joined me for a chat. He seemed a bit mixed-up in his feelings about the nation's economy, welcoming the business and prosperity, but uneasy about the stringent new work ethic that had come with it.

"Sure we're killin' ourselves to keep ourselves livin'," he concluded. "It's nearly enough to drive a man to the drink." He downed his whisky and laughed at his own whimsy. "I see you've been makin' the acquaintance of Danny Casey, one of Galway's own. There'd be no shortage of talkin', not with Danny about."

It quickly emerged that he'd been passing through the square earlier and had seen me and my 'ancient mariner' in conversation. Funny how the title of the poem suddenly came back to me. Mr Cassidy waited for a response from me. I felt uncomfortable, in view of the course our talk had taken, and offered some vague remark about Mr Casey being an interesting man. Cassidy still waited, expecting more, so I added a safe question. "Is he one of your guests in the hotel here?"

"Ah no, ah no, Danny drinks round in The Mermaid. You wouldn't get Danny drinkin' in here."

"I think we must be talking about two different people, Mr Cassidy. The man I was talking to doesn't drink, hasn't had a drink in over twenty years. He told me so himself."

"Did he now? And what else did he tell you?" The little man seemed more than casually interested, as though the information could have some bearing upon himself.

Still anxious not to betray a private conversation, I mentioned that my man was originally a fisherman from the Aran Islands. Cassidy gave an odd little smile. "I knew it, I knew it, he's in trainin'," he said, more to himself than to me. At that moment the barman from the front bar appeared with a tray of empty glasses. "You were right, Martin," Cassidy called over to him, "Casey's gettin' ready. He's goin' for the title this year again, as sure as there's a tail on a donkey."

The barman laughed. "Sure I told you that a week ago. I knew it the minute I heard him warmin' up on them Americans in The Mermaid last Wednesday. He'll be as hard to beat this year as ever, I'd say."

I was bewildered enough at this stage to abandon confidentiality and tell Cassidy everything else the man had told me, in the hope of an explanation. He listened intently to the whole thing - the marriage, accident, operations, tears, murders, the lot - his face a mixture of admiration and anxiety. When I'd finished he remarked, "He's back in top form, there's no denyin' that."

With a little prompting, I found out what was going on. Casey had been using me in his preparations for some obscure local title, The Liar of the West, a prestigious but, to outsiders, arcane annual competition, judged on the credibility and persuasiveness of its total lack of truthfulness. Not one word of Casey's story to me had been true. The man had never been closer to the Aran Islands than Galway Quay, knew nothing about fishing, or building, was unmarried, had never ridden a motorbike, was never in an accident or in hospital, had killed nobody, and drank like a fish.

Mr Cassidy was summing up. "Aye, he's got the gift, all right. It's a God-given gift he has. Still, he hasn't won the title now for three years, or is it four, and there's one or two other good runners in the field."

Cassidy's face wore an oblique little smile that was lost on me. "I won it meself the year before last," he confided, "and there's them that has their money on me for it this year again.

Before I forget, sir, we've the sea bass on this evenin'. They're grand, just in fresh this mornin', still slappin' and lookin' up at you out of the box. You've never tasted their equal."

That evening I chose the Chicken on a bed of puy lentils, with beetroot and a red wine sauce.

A BIT OF BAD LUCK

It was a good feeling, being the best, knowing he was the best. He allowed himself a little moment of self-satisfaction, checked he'd left nothing in the hotel room, and snapped shut the battered old brown suitcase.

That little moment was enough. He had never been one to dwell on his successes. Even when he'd been on the other side, working **for** H.M. Customs, he'd never joined fully in the backslapping celebrations among the Rummage Crews or Anti Smuggling Teams after a major seizure. Now, the classic gamekeeper turned poacher, he could feel the same quiet inner pride in avoiding detection as he had formerly felt in making it. As always, he kept the feeling to himself.

It wasn't just the risks in telling others of his superlative skills as a smuggler that kept him silent. He knew deep inside that any feelings of professional pride he might have were only sad little compensations for the true happiness he would never have again. Happiness for him had died the moment Denise had been murdered. Yes, murdered. *Tragic accident, terrible loss, cruel blow* - these all sidestepped the brutal truth that the police car had deliberately mounted the pavement in its pursuit of the stolen car and smashed her warm soft body so hard against the cold stone of the bridge that he wasn't allowed to identify her for more than an hour, until the mortuary people had made her presentable.

He shuddered each time the memory of that day threatened to force itself into his mind. That was the most cruel thing of all, that he couldn't even enjoy memories of the good times Denise and he had known. He had trained himself to shut them out. For the sake of his own sanity he did not dare allow himself memories of the person in the world he had loved most: they led inexorably to the terrible picture of her crushed form below a mortuary sheet, and the tormenting expression of mild surprise on her dead face.

It was something else, however, that had almost broken his reason, that had sent a whirling madness round and round in his head, in spite of the words of friends and colleagues, the work of doctors, counsellors, shrinks. It was the crass remark of that police officer in attendance at the identification that sent him to the verge of breakdown, and in due course reversed his entire life – *a bit of bad luck*. For weeks that phrase echoed inside his head, day after day, night after night, until it seemed that they were the only words that existed.

In desperation he had tried religion but could get from it none of the peace or comfort that some had supposed would be virtually guaranteed. What he did get, ironically, was a nudge in the direction of a new life, a life of crime, which was in time to stabilise his frantic mind through the therapy of hitting back.

He had noticed in his feverish rounds of the various churches and sects that many of the leaders, the pastors or priests or whatever they were called, were little nondescript men who in any other walk of life would almost certainly have been ignored or ridiculed. In this profession they enjoyed a deference and respect that nobody thought to challenge or question. It was as though they were a special case, not subject to the realities that ordinary people faced every day.

The observation took hold. He recalled parties of nuns passing through Customs on their way from Lourdes or some such holy place. There had been no shortage of crude remarks and jokes passed privately among the Assistant Officers about what might be found under the nuns' habits, or who might have already been there, but he had never seen a nun subjected to a close personal search, nor her baggage seriously 'turned out'.

A course of action started to firm up: he could turn his understanding of its thinking, his knowledge of its practice, against H.M. Customs, against 'authority', and the way to do it was in the guise of a man of the cloth.

He knew the idea was not a new one, that bogus clergymen had been rumbled before, but he would make deception an art form, he would take it to new heights. *A bit of bad luck?* No chance, luck wouldn't feature in his operations. Every precaution would be taken, every scenario would be anticipated, every challenge checkmated.......

It would soon be ten years since the nightmare time. In that period he had changed so utterly, in every respect, that he sometimes wondered who he was, and where and why, and if there ever had been a lovely, loving woman called Denise who had once been the best part of his life.

Irwin Davis was in a seriously grumpy mood. Quite apart from a throbbing wisdom tooth that his tongue refused to stop poking, and the row he'd had that morning with his wife after her old cat had peed inside one of his new shoes, there were larger matters behind the darkness of his face.

As H.M. Customs Surveyor he saw his work as a kind of trust, a charge, that denoted both character and ability. Declining detection or seizure figures in his Terminal, however slight, were, for Davis, a mark of personal weakness and failure. In spite of several recent successes that had seen a number of punters 'jobbed' and 'taken up the road' for cocaine and heroin charges, Davis's instinct told him that he was performing below his best; there was no evidence for this feeling, the statistics were relatively steady, but on previous occasions his instincts had proved to be correct.

He stared at his cup of cold coffee and shifted his mind into Overview Mode. Closing his eyes he pictured the large slogan their instructor had made the trainees recite each morning: *The jails are full of people who thought they were smarter than H.M. Customs.* Yes, but the job had changed a great deal over his thirty years of service. The game had got tougher, the players dirtier, the stakes higher, the rules trickier.

True, he could still net a fair catch by the standard means, the known profile methods, the credibility checks. The overly nervous or confident passenger was still worth a turn out. So too was the scruffy passenger bound for the expensive destination, or the punter with too little money for his intended stay, but they were no longer the whole story. Now the smuggler could be the smart businesswoman, the travelling wedding guests, the pretty young mother, the grandmother going out to see her grandchildren.

Was it just a sign of his age, or was he right in thinking that new staff coming into the job were less dedicated than in his day? Their plans for the weekend, or interest in salary scales, were just as important to them as detecting unlicensed importation or evasion of revenue duties. Even informers today were of inferior stuff. Davis smiled, in spite of his gloomy thoughts. A few days earlier an informer had reported that a corner shop was selling cigarettes at 60p. When his story was checked out it emerged courgettes were on sale at 60p. Maybe informers should be asked to sit a reading test.......

It was a lonely, humourless way of life he had chosen, a life of bare hotel rooms and colourless flats. How he used to enjoy coming home to share with Denise the incidents or gossip of the day. She had smiled to herself all evening at his account of the drug carrier caught by declaring he was on his way to take up a job as a barman in Pakistan, an Islamic 'dry' country. He had hurried home another day to tell her of the armed police reception for two men overheard to be arriving from Ireland with armalite guns, but in fact travelling with nothing more dangerous than Carmelite nuns. She had laughed out loud over the passenger who, told he would have to go with his bag to the gate, had thrown his suitcase onto the belt, sat astride it, and ridden off through the curtains to the sorting area below.

Now, no matter how exciting or interesting his day might be, there was nobody he dared trust enough to tell it to. The only way to keep his secret was to tell nobody, literally nobody. A person sworn to secrecy will tell just one other person; that one other person in turn tells just one other, who then tells only one other, and so it goes until the secret is public knowledge. He remembered with a wry smile how a friend had once told him about an affair he was having, adding, "Now, I don't want you to tell anybody, not even Denise. Promise." What an innocent. Anybody who thinks for a minute that a husband will keep a piece of juicy news secret from his wife is too naïve for words. No, the only thing you can't tell is what you don't know.

A dog was barking below his hotel window. The racket reached him above the noise of people and traffic in the busy Bogota street. Why did all these foreign towns and cities always have a dog barking somewhere, in the distance or right outside the window. Sometimes the barking would waken him from a dream in which a detector dog had been announcing a find. Strange, but even now, more than eight years since he'd switched sides, his dreams were still of those early days, or rather nights, the late night Baggage Watch on the Green Channels, when he would search the holds and cabins of aircraft and ships, or carry out tarmac and dockside challenges.

He took the lift down to the hotel lobby, checked out, and, even though his flight was not due for take-off for three hours, took a taxi out to the Eldorado International Airport. He told the driver to drive slowly. He hated fast driving.

He caught a glimpse of his face in the driver's mirror. It was a face unrecognisable from the round, bearded one that used to belong to a man who worked as an Assistant Officer for H.M. Customs. This face was lean, grey, clean-shaven, with a kind of gravitas in the lined forehead and in the serious eyes behind the gold-rimmed spectacles. The hair, once thick and strong, was now a thin distinguished white, combed back in a widow's peak and neatly trimmed above the clerical collar.

He had destroyed all photographs of himself and of his former life, and could scarcely believe that he had once been a 'heavy' of fifteen stone. Three of these had vanished virtually overnight during his illness after Denise's death, and his subsequent new lifestyle had reduced him further to the present 150 pounds filling his neat dark suit.

The priest persona was used only for 'work'. For the rest of the time he presented a very different appearance. Crouched inside a donkey jacket and wearing a beanie over straggly grey hair, he showed an unshaven face and coarse moustache. He enjoyed the contrast in his two roles. It was a kind of game, but never a game of chance. The gains he made, which were considerable, were his reward for winning the game, but it was the playing of it that mattered. He controlled the play, he didn't need luck. Why gamble, when he could load the dice in his own favour. He kept away, for example, from his former place of employment. His disguise was good, but why put it to the unnecessary test of customs men who had known him in his former life.

He patted the suitcase beside him on the shabby leather seat. It was a relic from the fifties, chosen deliberately to underline his unworldliness. He would sometimes catch snide remarks from the Customs Officers about 'demob' and 'old Blighty' as they gave it a cursory check. Inside were more targets for the wits; old-fashioned underpants, the type that used to be known as trunks, backed up by long johns; a large face flannel enclosing a bar of Lifebuoy soap; Aertex singlets; a pair of suspenders to support the long black socks; a pair of broad elastic garters to hold up the sleeves of the white clerical shirts; a clothes brush worn almost smooth by years of honest service; a shaving brush with an equally busy history.

Together with these carefully chosen items were the cassock and various trappings of the priest, and a selection of religious leaflets, pamphlets and booklets. The centrepiece of the suitcase's contents was a large, well-used bible, its leather covers almost as worn as the seat it now sat on. This was his moneymaker, his livelihood.

Just after he had started work as an AO he had been asked to turn out the baggage of an elderly clergyman, and at the time had felt a little uncomfortable as he poked among the contents of the old fellow's bag, especially flicking through his bible and ecclesiastical books. It was the same kind of feeling he still got when pulling out in a hurry to overtake an ambulance or funeral procession. Talking about it afterwards to hardened searchers he was surprised to learn that they could feel that same sense of impropriety.

"I'm not a religious man," one of them had said, "but I try to respect a man who is."

He had remembered those words as with infinite patience he doctored the bible, slicing its thin pages with a surgeon's scalpel and with a surgeon's skill. It was ' the oldest trick in the book' quite literally, but the care he took in distributing the little incised boxes at precisely calculated distances and positions throughout the bible occupied him for the best part of a week. The result was a book that could be loosely skimmed through, with no evidence at all of the series of cavities hidden between its pages. So expertly were the pages sealed that a casual flick through them produced the wholly natural appearance of the leaves of a book turning over in random sections.

Nothing was left to chance. He had weighed the bible before operating on it, and was methodical in ensuring that the gemstones or gold tola bars he implanted in its secret niches did not make it noticeably heavier than it should have been. At no time did his Good Book's pages carry drugs; dogs didn't make any allowances for men in round white collars.

The airport lounge was relatively slack. He chose a seat in a corner and hid behind a newspaper. A priest was an invitation. On one occasion someone had taken a fatal heart attack just before boarding and he had been summoned to administer the last rites. It was a measure of his preparations for his new career that he had envisaged just such a situation and was able to act it out with 'professional' assurance, before slipping away through the crowd.

On another occasion he had the misfortune to have beside him on the plane a chirpy young curate, or some such apprentice, who was all set for intercontinental conversation. He had put a quick stop to that nonsense. From the gold nib of his old style fountain pen flowed the words *I'm terribly sorry, but at present I'm forbidden to speak. I'm on my way to have an operation for my throat cancer.* The curate squeezed himself into the far side of his seat. Cancer's not contagious, but............

Davis took his cup down to the staff kitchen. On the way back he looked in at the Staff Room. An Officer and three Assistant Officers were playing poker before their watch started. They were in the process of recovering from a burst of laughing.

"What's amusing you lot?"

The Officer was pleased to get the question. "I've just been telling them about what happened yesterday. It's true, I swear it's true. I was helping an American Captain to fill in his crew declaration, and he was asking me about the tobacco products column. I told him to list any tobacco or fags he had on board and, I swear it's true, he wrote down, 'The Chief Steward, but I'm not certain.' I swear it's true."

All four greeted the punch line with renewed merriment, and Davis conceded an amused nod.

"I swear something else is true," he said. "I've been looking at the figures. We've challenged more punters and turned out more baggage in the past month than any other Terminal, and we're still at the bottom of the table for arrests and seizures. Now, what does that tell you?"

One of the AO's looked up from shielding his hand. "Maybe it's telling us we're the best. Maybe we should be top of the table, the deterrent table. Maybe our reputation's doing the business."

Davis wanted to say something witty and withering in reply, but couldn't deliver. The card game resumed. It annoyed him to see their apparent lack of concern. His thoughts turned bitter. Perhaps they were right in their outlook, and he was the one with things out of focus. Maybe the truth was that their work was no different than their game of poker. Both depended to a very large extent on luck: pulling the right card, picking the right passenger. Was there any difference? Maybe all their training and planning came right down to that, the luck of the draw, the throw of the dice, and he was having a bad run. Were all his training and knowledge and experience, were all the established procedures and methods, worth no more than the chance choice of a card?

Davis felt his mind slide from dark to black; he found himself thinking about having the cat put down............

The flight was as boring as the countless others he had made in his work. A little rebellious part of him occasionally hoped for a hijacking or some kind of drama on board, but he knew such thoughts were dangerously unprofessional.

He politely declined the drink the hostess offered him. As a teenager, in another life centuries ago, he had thought of air hostesses as having one of the most glamorous jobs in the world; now he pitied them, wheeling their trolleys endlessly up and down narrow aisles, issuing safety advice nobody listened to, sorting out the needs and mistakes of incredibly stupid people, and all the time having to smile and be pleasant. It would be better being a waitress in a corner café.

He liked the Colombian run. It was a popular target for drug searches, which relied quite a bit on the dogs for detections. It wasn't a route that Customs associated with the smuggling of commercial gemstones. In reply to the familiar, "Where have you travelled from today?" he would try to include biblical or 'churchy' words, if possible, in his replies. They were a guaranteed turn-off. A *Convocation* or *Synod* or *Ecclesiastical Council* would produce almost instant glazing of the eyes.

He checked his passport. Perfect, undetectable. He should know. He got a new one each year from the best forger in the business. It was worth the two grand. Too many entry stamps, especially of dicey countries, drew attention.

That was why he was the best - he could second-guess the opposition. How he despised the raw, desperate amateurs, the swallowers and stuffers, the couple who split up to go through controls separately.....

For Irwin Davis brooding was a positive thing, the first stage in a process that led to decisions, whether right ones or wrong ones. He emptied his cup and strode purposefully back down to the Staff Room, arriving just as the poker game was finishing.

"Wait a minute, Arthurs," he intervened as the deck was being put in its box. "Let me cut the pack." He got the four of clubs.

"Ah, the devil's bedposts," remarked Arthurs, who was a walking encyclopaedia of just such useless facts. "Unlucky for some."

"OK. That's it. Number 4. When you lot go on duty I want you to turn out, and I mean turn out, every fourth passenger coming through. I don't care if it's the queen or the pope or your own mother, I want them checked over, right down to the gold in their teeth." There were a few murmurs from the team. "I don't care how long it takes. The public think we do random stops anyway, so for today let's prove them right. Turn out every fourth punter as if you know for sure he's carrying the Crown Jewels."

His old suitcase was one of the first out at Baggage Reclaim. As always, after hours in a planeload of humanity, he looked forward to the privacy and independence of his own car in the Long Stay Car Park. Fortunately there were only three other passengers in front of him as he entered the Customs Control area............

BEN

I mistrust those good-luck happy ending stories that surface every now and again: the last 10p that hits the jackpot; the idle lottery ticket purchase that scoops a fortune, usually for some down-and-outer; the careless cast, at the end of an empty day, that reels in a 25 pounder. In my experience, the final cast is more likely to snag on a branch and lose me my best fly or spinner.

Maybe it's something to do with personality, this luck business, and yes, I've always found it easier to brood over a failure than to celebrate a success. Some psychologists claim that being lucky is largely a matter of feeling lucky. I wonder what they would have made of Ben Perry.

Ben and I lay like bookends at the bottom end of the ward, my right arm and shoulder encased in plaster, his left counterparts matching them in the next bed. There had been no element of bad luck in my injury, just stupidity. I had that hedge trimmed as neat as a wall and should have left it at that but, hungry for praise, I got back up the stepladder to snip a solitary rogue leaf. Next thing I was in a heap on the ground with a compound fracture of the right arm.

Now Ben's case was very different. With no fault of any kind on his part, he had found himself with a shattered left shoulder. Somebody had dropped a heavy glass ashtray from a top window of a downtown building, and Ben had shouldered the consequences - comminuted fractures of the left clavicle and scapula, as the surgeon had explained to him before his three-hour operation.

Ben repeated the phrase to me with pride. "Aye, comminuted fractures of the left clavicle and scapula. Man but I'm the lucky boy. Another inch or two to the right and I'd be dead meat." He downed a glass of lucozade.

While I could easily appreciate the narrowness of his escape, I knew that in his position I would have been moaning, "Why me?"

Ben was in his late fifties, a large man with long delicate fingers that seemed not to belong to him, like the man in the old horror film with someone else's hands grafted on. He was really tickled when I introduced myself as William.

"William? Bill? You're Bill, I'm Ben. Bill and Ben, get it?" For him that made us instant friends.

Ben liked to talk. I offered him a tabloid newspaper our first morning together on the ward and he read the huge headline that occupied the front page. With his working hand he turned the paper over on the bed and scanned the back page.

"That's it read, cover to cover." He laughed at his own wit as he handed the paper back into my working left hand. Fortunately our beds were so placed that our good hands were adjacent, although the main things exchanged between us were words.

Exchanged is hardly the right term. Ben was one of those people who tell everything, personal matters, financial situation, private concerns, so that I started to feel guilty hearing all his affairs, and offered back a few items of my own to keep the scales from tipping over completely.

He was divorced, on the grounds of what the judge had termed 'hopeless incompatibility', and lived on the small savings he had from the Merchant Navy and a disability pension following a freak accident. A parked car had suddenly taken off and crushed his thighs against the bumper of a van parked in front.

"Lucky I'm a tall kinda fella," he grinned across to me, "or it woulda been the crown jewels that got it. Bill and Ben, that's a good 'un right enough, Bill and Ben. Tell you what, I've two pot plants at home. I'll get our Gerry to bring them in and we'll put them beside the beds."

It emerged that Gerry was Ben's twin brother. Gerry Perry - good thinking, mum and dad. The first time he visited the ward it never occurred to me for a moment that he was Ben's twin brother. I've sometimes heard people marvelling at how alike identical twins can be; this pair was even more remarkable. There was not one single feature that would have suggested they were related at all, let alone twin brothers. Gerry's small frame, tightly curled dark hair, worried expression and nervy manner were all in complete contrast to his brother's easygoing appearance and disposition. Ben was pleased to tell me afterwards that he was an hour younger than Gerry, and the 'baby' of the family.

When Gerry arrived at the bedside early next morning it wasn't flowerpots he brought with him. I knew at once there was something wrong: words like 'missing' and 'police' reached me from the urgent communication next door. Ben listened, but from what I could see past the edge of my paper, showed none of the reactions his brother's earnest narration might have expected.

Once he had delivered his bulletin in suitably private manner, Gerry was free to go public. He suddenly turned to me, a stranger, and repeated it, hoping perhaps for better audience response.

"He's been done. Cleaned. Last night. Happened last night. I couldn't believe it. Goes down this mornin' to feed Rambo for him and knows right away. The front door's lyin' open, and Rambo comes out waggin' his tail. Couldn't believe it. Place is stripped – TV, video, microwave, the lot. Calls the police. What do they say - they're sendin' somebody over this afternoon, after three. I'm to make a list of everythin' that's missin'. How am I expected to make a list? Couldn't believe it. He can't do it, lyin' in here."

'He' was listening to the account again, from a third party point of view.

"No, couldn't believe it. I stands there, just stands there. You shoulda seen me. Here was me." He produced for me the pantomime of a man completely flabbergasted, eyes wide in disbelief, mouth sagging in shock.

The focus of the story had shifted from the burglary to the degree of Gerry's incredulity, and I was trying to make the right noises in response to his performance, when 'he' suddenly broke in.

"They've missed the car. They didn't get the car. Now there's a lucky one. I have her in for a new gearbox. You remember I'd just left her in, Gerry, and was walkin' back when I got hit by the ashtray. No, I've come outa this not too bad, they didn't get the car.........."

The one thing Gerry did have in common with his twin was a fondness for talking. He called back that same afternoon, this time with the pot plants, which the burglars in their wisdom had chosen to leave behind. Ben had been taken down for tests, so he favoured me with the visit. We discussed his brother's condition and progress.

"Does his wife not come to see him?" I asked mischievously. The result was startling: I had accidentally pushed the Ben Perry biography button, and out tumbled a life history of bad luck, accident, mischance, call it what you will. I managed to steer Gerry to the marital misfortune chapter.

"It was never gonna work, never. I knew from day one. She had no patience, y'see, and the thing you need most with our Ben is patience.

Things started goin' wrong right from the honeymoon, would you believe. He went through a Car Wash and forgot he had put the neighbour's roof rack on for their suitcases. Their clothes were ruined. So was the roof rack. She couldn't say too much, she hadn't remembered the roof rack either, but it was a sample of what was to come.

To tell you the truth, it was only Ben bein' away on the boats that kept them together, if you see what I mean. They nearly split up the very first time he came home to her from the Merchant Navy.

He'd been away about five months or so, gettin' fifty quid a month and bags of overtime, and he'd saved it all, about four hundred and fifty quid, which was big money in them days. He shoulda been sendin' it home every month, but she was workin' and was OK. He told me he was plannin' to come back with enough to change the car.

Anyway, he gets off at Liverpool with a day in hand and decides to go down to Manchester to see a mate. He has all his money wrapped in an elastic band in the breast pocket of his boiler jacket. What does he do? He's passin' the Manchester Ship Canal and starts lookin' over the bridge at the ships goin' through. You can see what's comin'. As he's leanin' over, the roll gets pushed up out of the pocket, and five months' money goes over the edge and down into the water. She done her nut when he got home penniless."

"Terrible, terrible. Did she not feel sorry for him at all?"

Gerry allowed himself a tired smile. "It's hard to feel sorry for a man who doesn't feel sorry for himself. That's why I don't blame her maybe as much as I should. You'd need to be a saint to live with our Ben. I couldn't do it. Everything seems to happen to him. The funny thing is, it never seems to fizz on him."

Gerry went on to recount a series of further mishaps, some of them, but only some, of Ben's own making. I kept thinking during the recital that any one of them would have been enough to put me under.

How would I have coped if starlings had slyly built a nest in my chimney, filling my best room with black smoke and covering the new carpet with a layer of soot the first time I lit the fire. What if a cat had somehow got below my house to die, and I had had to rip up the floorboards in two rooms to locate the source of the terrible stench. Suppose I had accidentally flushed a towel down the loo, blocking the pipe, so that the whole length of the recently laid tarmacadam driveway had to be dug up.

"What finished them off?" I asked Gerry, whose tone throughout had implied fault on Ben's part, even when things were beyond anybody's control.

"It was the whole Australian thing that done it." Gerry shook his head in sad wisdom, like a man who can foresee disaster but is powerless to prevent it. "He was drivin' her down to Dublin airport to go out to see her sister in Australia. I got the whole story from him and her both.

Ben had tidied out the car and packed in her luggage. Somewhere on the other side of Newry the car started to wobble. They'd got a puncture. That's when the fun started. Ben had set the spare wheel out of the boot when he was tidyin' the car, and left it sittin' in the garage. Easy done, I suppose, but I wouldna' done it. I check everythin'. Anyway, Ben calms her down and says, 'We're in luck, we've got the foot pump.' From there the whole way to Dublin they was stoppin' every ten minutes for Ben to blow up the soft tyre, and her gettin' more and more panicky, and lookin' at her watch and screamin' at Ben, and him tellin' her they'd be all right.

Would you believe, after all them capers they missed the plane only by five minutes. Her sister at the other end had already set out to drive about six hundred mile to meet her. That was the last straw. She put him out, and he moved to where he is now, the bungalow. I think it was him admirin' the scenery in the middle of all them antics on the Dublin road that overturned the applecart for good...........'"

I was discharged before Ben. We went through the usual 'keep in touch' routine, but I wasn't expecting to see much more of him, unless by chance. He insisted I take the pot plant with me 'as a souvenir'.

I was surprised, and excited in some undefined way, when I answered the phone about four months later and heard, "Bill? It's Ben. Us flowerpot men has to stick together."

Ben's spell in hospital had been longer than anyone had expected. Some of the bone fragments had knitted wrongly, and he needed further surgery.

"Really sorry to hear that, Ben. If I'd known you were still in I'd have come over to see you."

"Not to worry, not to worry. Two for the price of one: buy one and get one free, so to speak. Tell you why I'm ringin', Bill. I've moved house. Aye, I've sold the bungalow. Couldn't hold out to the mortgage repayments. Sold her and paid off the mortgage in one go. I've bought a nice wee terrace house in Morrissey Street. Suits me well, garden and all at the back.

You remember, Bill, you mentioned you had a car trailer? I was wonderin' if I could borrow it this Saturday mornin'. Tell you what for." He gave a little giggle. "The man who's bought the bungalow is just off the phone to me. He doesn't want my wee shed at the back, and he's givin' it to me for the takin' away." Another little giggle. "Would the trailer be free on Saturday mornin' for a coupla hours?"

I arranged to meet Ben at the bungalow, bring the trailer, and give him a hand on with the shed. The morning was fine but a little gusty. I noticed for the first time his odd clockwork walk, no doubt the result of his argument with the runaway car.

I had expected the shed to be taken apart ready for removal, but there it sat, empty and forlorn. It was one of those self-assembly light alloy things, sold in Garden Centres and D.I.Y. stores.

"We'll take her as she is. We'll set her on and tie her down. It's only a few mile into town. We'll be able to carry her round the back and set her over the hedge."

Ben rubbed his hands together in anticipation of the finished job.

I was following along behind towards the town, the shed riding pretty astride the trailer, when without warning it suddenly leapt straight up into the air as from a springboard, executed a perfect double somersault with pike and tuck, and dived out of sight behind a hedge. Ben was driving along contentedly, elbow out the window, admiring the scenery. I flashed the lights to inform him that he was pulling an empty trailer.

The shed lay in the field, a crumpled mess, the detached door stuck in the mud like a wafer in a chocolate sundae.

"Lucky she went over the hedge," said Ben, his inspection completed. "She coulda caused an accident." For once I shared entirely his feeling of good fortune.

We rolled the shed up and crammed it into the boot of Ben's car. A pointed piece protruded. Bill went back into the field and returned with a large stone.

"We're in luck," he grinned, and battered the point flat. The boot lid just about clicked shut at the third slam. Bill expelled a sigh of relief. "She's in. Lucky enough." I had to comment. "I notice, Ben, you don't seem to let things get you down."

He thought about it for a moment or two. "Well, it's like this: somethin' really bad could happen tomorrow, and then I'd be wishin' I was back here the way I am now."

I was to see Ben twice more. In September freak rainfall flooded several streets in the old part of the town, and as soon as I heard Morrissey Street on the news broadcast I knew what to expect. The pictures showed people in wellington boots wading through brownish water.

I drove down the rainwashed road to town and parked a few streets away from the flooded area. The rain had stopped and the water had receded, leaving behind a sorry scene. Sodden sandbags had been pulled away to allow mud to be slopped out of doors, and there was a telltale tidemark just below the window sills.

"Bill? What're you doin' down here? How you doin', how's it goin'?" Ben slithered over to me in thigh waders, really pleased to see me. We shook hands.

"It's awful this...terrible...terrible."

Ben agreed it was bad, wasn't sure how he stood insurance-wise, and wondered if he should 'put her on the market.' I imagined his advertisement - *Would suit first time buyers with an interest in water sports* or *Ample parking space for rowing boat.* Finally he added, "C'mon round the back. I've somethin' to show you."

Sitting at the end of a cinder path, close beside a small greenhouse, was a construction unlike anything I'd ever seen before. It looked like a large packing case clad in a battered corrugated tin coat. At first I wasn't sure what I was being invited to admire, but then the sickly cream of the crinkled coating gave me the clue.

"The shed."

"Aye, the shed, the new improved version. I got her rolled back out and nailed her on. Got the pallets for nothin' up at the skip." Ben gave that distinctive little giggle. "She's like new, far stronger, better than new."

February was the hardest for half a century, temperatures way below zero, people talking about nothing but the weather and how to keep warm. I came in from scraping ice off the windscreen to find a message on the answer phone: *Hya, Bill. It's Ben. Bit cold for us flowerpot men. How's the arm? Is the cold gettin' to it? Listen, if you get a chance come down some day and bring the trailer. No, I'm not movin' another shed, I've somethin' for you. There'll be no floodin' this time, I hope. Do your best to get down, Bill. Cheerio.*

Ben sounded in top spirits. Curiosity drove me down that afternoon to Morrissey Street. Ben came to the door and when I saw how pleased he was to see me I was glad I had accepted his invitation. We chatted briefly, Ben all the time holding some inner satisfaction in check.

"Come on through to the back," and he led me through the kitchen into the long narrow garden.

The tree lay sprawled over the grass, crushing bushes, smothering the pathway. First victims of the fall had been the greenhouse and the 'new, improved' shed, both smashed by the main trunk of the fallen giant.

I was on the point of offering sympathy for the losses when Ben released a little giggle of excitement and turned me towards the far side of the kitchen, where it extended into the garden. Behind it, in neat rows, was a pile of tidy stove length logs, stacked like gold bullion.

"These are for you, Bill. They'll keep the old flowerpot warm. Take as many as you want. There'll be plenty more where they came from," and he gestured towards the huge fallen tree. He rubbed his hands together in pleasure. "The man next door has a chainsaw and he's cuttin' her up for me. Nice bit of luck, especially in this cold weather. You need a bit of luck now and again............."

PLAY OFF

How had she always imagined panic to be something quick and dramatic - *panic stricken, sudden panic, panic attack.* The feeling that had invaded her was stealthy and steady, but it was panic just the same. It had probably been working away in secret for some time, but she could pinpoint the exact moment the actual occupation began.

Brenda and she had met in town for lunch and were having the usual natter afterwards over a gin and tonic.

"That's the difference between you and me, Pat. You're too trusting. If Ross were my husband I wouldn't let him away on all these golf outings and weekend things. He could be seeing somebody else, for all you know."

Pat returned the serve neatly: "I read somewhere that the best way to lose a man is to chain him up." It was at that very moment, as she delivered the little epigram, that the panic, which was now her daily companion, made its move. Into her mind slid the realisation that she couldn't have cared less whether her husband was having an affair or not. In fact, it would have been almost a kind of relief to learn that he was being unfaithful.

The beachhead was established, and panic's infiltration began from that quiet recognition - she didn't love Ross then, probably never had loved him, and, worst of all, was almost repelled by him.

That first flare of insight lit up the poor wreckage of Pat Walker's thirty four years of life. She had achieved none of the dreams that had vaguely coloured her early ambitions: no special talents or accomplishments, no qualifications or career in Art and Design, no circle of good friends, no children. Her one apparent success, marriage to a young handsome husband, was a lie. Ross had done well from the marriage, acquiring social status and business opportunity, but from Pat's point of view the relationship had deteriorated so rapidly that she could hardly believe she was married at all.

Pat's sense of panic burned deeper each time she looked ahead, but instead of consuming itself in a fierce blaze, it smouldered and took even firmer hold. The only picture that appeared on the screen of her future was a fuzzy one of empty middle age...

Pat poured herself a very generous gin, splashed in a suggestion of tonic, and returned to the couch. She could hear Ross rattling his clubs together in the hallway. The sound irritated her. Everything about him irritated her, right down to those little vulgar habits she had once overlooked or tried to find amusing: dipping biscuits in his tea was well up the list, but personal things too, like the way he put his tongue out like a budgie's when he coughed, were now unbearable.

"That's me away. I should be back about six or seven on Sunday." He didn't come into the room.

"Cheerio." Pat didn't have to try to sound dry; she would have found it impossible to put any warmth in her voice.

"If any calls come for me..."

"I'll make a note of them — name, time, number, message, if any. I know my duties by now."

He fired up instantly, and came in from the hall, two little telltale points of red high in his cheeks. "Don't start all that again. You're becoming tiresome. Sometimes I really think you're jealous of me - you don't like to see me enjoying myself. I wouldn't object if you were going away for a few days to enjoy yourself."

"No, you'd welcome it. It's not so long since you were swearing you could enjoy nothing without me. To think I believed all that stuff. How did I not see through it?"

Ross was about to enter into the fray but he thought better of it and went out with the clubs, slamming the outside door as he left. She heard the Volvo roaring off in a rage.

Pat felt no satisfaction from the skirmish, just a sad little pleasure in seeing again that his hair was definitely starting to grey at the sides. How had things been reduced to this. What was that phrase she had heard at school that had somehow stuck in her mind – something about people leading lives of quiet desperation. The words had meant little to her then, but they were bang on target now.

She emptied her glass, hardly tasting the drink. Pat's affair with alcohol was a volatile one; it could sink her into melancholy or spark her into friskiness, all in an instant. The school thought suddenly reminded her of Brenda and their arrangement, and in a moment she was dialling her, excited and girlish.

"Brenda. He's away. Bring your own nightie this time."

Brenda. Now there was a real person. When everyone and everything else let her down, there was Brenda. How would she have coped without her one true friend. She felt momentarily ashamed of all those times she had been aware of her natural and social superiority; yes, Pat was prettier and from a better background, but never once had her pal shown even a hint of jealousy or resentment. She blushed that even now, in the midst of her remorse and gratitude, the feeling still persisted that however bad things might be for her, they were worse for Brenda. Could that be what friends were for? Pat fixed herself another drink to ward off the bad thought...

Brenda came in brandishing a bottle of wine in each hand. "Da Daaaa... The best that Tesco can supply at £4.99 a bottle."
Pat laughed. "I want to drink the stuff, not cook with it."
Brenda unhooked her shoulder bag and made straight for the drinks cupboard. "Give me a Gordons, quick. That stuff I've been buying tastes like ivy juice."
"It's great to see you, Brenda. Thanks for coming over."
"Sure, but what are your neighbours saying? Every time Ross goes off with his clubs, hey presto, I'm on your doorstep in a flash. It looks like classic *Golf Widow and her Lesbo Lover* stuff."
Pat was already on a high, just having Brenda with her. "Frankly, my dear, I don't give a damn," she drawled. "No suh, instead ahm gonna have me a gin and It."
"Tell you what, you have the gin and give me the It. I've been looking for It all week."
Pat giggled, Brenda laughed at Pat giggling, and the evening was off and running....

"No, it's true, Brenda, and I'm speaking from expense, sorry, experience, or maybe I was right the first time, but anyway, believe me, any man who marries up always resents it, and any woman who marries down is never sure, never completely sure, if she's been married for herself or for her money..."

"All right, so I'm a little tiddly, or my voice is a little tiddly, but my mind's as clear as a nun's diary – Ross knows what he stands to lose, so he'd better ship up, or shape out, or something like that."
"Promise me this, Pat, and I want it in writing. If he goes on the market, I get first refusal. You can have my flexible friend as commission"

"What I'd like, and who wouldn't, is a secure relationship and a bit on the side. At the moment I've neither."
"Don't be greedy. I'd settle for either."
"You know what I like most about you, Brenda – you never change."
Pat knew that part of her was fairly drunk, but she was surprised how clearly she was thinking and articulating her thoughts. "Maybe it's all our own fault. We make

men too important in our lives. Remember at school we always had to have a boyfriend, whether we liked him or not. It was social death not to have a boyfriend. I want you to do something for me, Brenda, just for a minute. Think back on those days, go on, think back on them, and tell me the truth – where did all the good times, the good laughs, the really good laughs, come from? From us, from ourselves, that's where from, without boys or men or whatever you want to call them, only we didn't know it at the time. Wait a minute, maybe you did, and that's why you stayed single."

Brenda laughed. "I hadn't much choice in the matter, and I can't say I've been laughing ever since. No, you're right, I have to agree, we did have some good laughs in those days. Remember we all bought those stupid tee shirts with our names on the front, and you had PAT in big letters right across your breasts?"

"Yes, and nobody took up the offer. And they were good breasts too. Still are. Breasts. Doesn't that sound old-fashioned? Nowadays girls just talk about their tits. I'm not sure if I like that or not."

Pat emptied her glass and set it on the glass-topped table. Her tone modulated: "I'm serious when I tell you this, Brenda, I'm laughing but I'm serious – a good friend, a really good friend, is worth half a dozen husbands, and you're the best friend anybody could have, so how many husbands must you be worth?"

She picked up her empty glass and drank from it. Brenda seemed moved by the compliment but hid it in a joke. "This sounds to me like a coming out. Maybe the neighbours have something to gossip about after all. Either that, or else you're like one of those stupid men who go all slobbery when they get a few drinks in."

Pat didn't reply and Brenda, perhaps feeling she might have hurt her, abruptly changed the subject.

"Oh, nearly forgot, guess who I saw in Stanton on Wednesday."

Pat snorted. "Guess who I saw in Stanton on Wednesday – the daft things people say. There's just about ten thousand million people out there, and I'm expected to guess who you saw in Stanton on Wednesday. Hold on a minute, I'll just nip out and win the lottery. O.K., game on, but you'll have to give me a clue. Male or female?"

"Male."

"Male – I love him already. Married or single?"

"Don't know. I'm tired of this game. It was Tony Taylor."

Pat looked up from twirling her empty glass. Her face was heavy and the mouth a little slack, but her eyes were bright and focused.

"Tony Taylor? The Tony Taylor from school?"

"Yessir, the same, the Tony Taylor from school. He's the only one I know."

"Are you sure it was him? I mean, it must be over twenty years since we saw him."

"It was him all right. I was stopped at traffic lights and he walked right across in front of the car. Definite, sure."

"Tony Taylor – I can't believe it. He was goodlooking in a dark Christopher Lee kind of way. Saturnine."

Brenda gave a little laugh. "Saturnine. That's a good word. I'm sure Tony Taylor would be pleased to know that at this very minute somebody is describing him as saturnine. He'd probably be delighted to know he's being talked about at all."

"Did I ever tell you I went out with him once?" and a strange little thrill of satisfaction ran through Pat when she saw Brenda's look of surprise.

"What? Now the secrets are coming out. You told me in about fourth form that you fancied him, but you never said anything about actually going out with him."

Pat got up and opened another bottle of wine. She was tempted for a moment to dress the story up but, prompted by laziness, she opted for the facts.

"There's nothing to tell. The whole thing was a damp squib, or soaking wet squib might be better. He took me to the pictures, the old Tivoli. We didn't hold hands, we didn't even talk. Funny, I can remember what the film was – *Halloween* – I nearly peed myself with fear. Then he walked me home and the rain came on. That was the beginning and end of the big romance. Never even kissed me. I remember wondering afterwards why he'd asked me out at all."

Brenda digested the account and pronounced judgement. "Taylor was always a bit weird. I'm surprised he didn't bite you in the neck."

"What, weird because he didn't kiss me?" Pat laughed.

"That too. I meant taking you on a first date to a film like that. He's scarier than the movie."

They sat in silence for a few minutes, rethinking the past. Finally Pat said, "All right, maybe so, but he was interesting, if you know what I mean, and I bet he doesn't play golf and try to impress other people. I wonder what he does, where he lives, if he's got any little Christopher Lee look-alikes."

"Maybe he's just normal and has a gay live-in lover," said Brenda, breaking the spell.

Pat took a thoughtful sip of wine. "Isn't it funny how all the people you used to see every day disappear and you never find out what's become of them? I'd love to know how some of the people in our year turned out."

Brenda had been studying a table lamp through her red wine when she suddenly set the glass down and turned to her friend with the old familiar note of schoolgirl excitement in her voice. "Why don't we find out? What's the term they use – run a check? We could run a check on your friend Mr Taylor. Find out where he lives, stalk him. Yes, that's it, that's all the rage, stalk him. We could have a laugh like the old times, instead of shopping our brains out."

For a moment Pat was back behind the Art Hut for an illegal smoke, planning to mitch hockey or some other stunt, but she touched the brakes of her feelings and remarked, "You're loopy, you know that, genuinely loopy. I'm the one who's drunk most of the wine, and I'm making more sense than you are."

"But why not? We'd be great stalkers. We need a bit of excitement, both of us. Think of the headlines: *Stanton Man in Stalking Terror.*"

"Or *Sex Starved Women Sought in Stanton Stalking Storm.*" The voice was Pat's, her face flushed with wine and excitement. "But where would we start?"

"Some are born to lead, and some are born to be led. Aren't you lucky I'm one of the leaders. Where's the phone book? There can't be too many Tony Taylors living in Stanton. I'll just look up all the T. Taylors and check them out. I'll know his voice right away."

Pat shook her head in resigned amusement. "The great leader's an illiterate. It'll be A. Taylor, not T. Anthony, you ignoramus. Wait a minute, we used to call him Rat, do you remember? R.A.T. Richard Anthony Taylor."

Brenda was already leafing through the directory, keeping Pat at bay. "Hold on, hold on, you're forgetting I wasn't in your class. You stay over there, or you'll make me laugh and give the game away. Taylor R., Taylor R., Taylor Robin, Taylor R.A.. There it is, there's only one R.A. It must be him. Taylor R.A., 28 Treadle Avenue, Stanton."

"Treadle Avenue? Doesn't sound too impressive, does it?" Pat felt vaguely disappointed that he had been located so easily, preferring him as a fancy in her imagination to a street name, a house number. "Arise, Sir Anthony, Lord of Treadle. Let me see."

"No, get off, go away, you're going to spoil this before it gets started."

Brenda dialled carefully from the book. "Hold on, hold on, it's ringing. …Hello, I'd like to book a table for four for this evening, please…What? Oh, sorry, sorry, beg your pardon… It's him, it's him, it's definitely him, I'd know that creepy voice anywhere."

"It's not creepy, it's silky, you Philistine. So what now?"

Brenda closed the phone book in triumph, and reached for the wine. "First thing, we'll finish this, then we'll get a good night's sleep, bypass the shops in the morning, and it's straight on for Stanton, the ancestral seat of Sir Anthony. We can take a picnic and do a stakeout like the cops in the movies. I've always wondered what they do when they need a pee."

"You're impossible. I know what's going to happen in the morning. We'll end up in Sainsburys buying Brie and broccoli…"

"Treadle Avenue.... Treadle Avenue...let me see." The man screwed up his face to assist the process. "O.K., you'll have to turn back and.... Treadle Avenue? No, wait a minute, you're all right.... You see them traffic lights where that red lorry's turnin' in. Go you on through and take the second, no, the third, yes, the third, the third street on your left. You'll come to a big roundabout. Go straight through and take the first on the left, no, it'll be right goin' this way, yes, the first on your right. You'll see a big church on the corner. You'll come then to another set of lights. Go left and about three or four hundred yards down on the right you'll see Treadle Road. Treadle Avenue would be the third, or maybe the next one down, on the left, off Treadle Road. You couldn't miss it."

"Did you get all that?" Brenda asked, keeping her expression earnest.

"Great. The whole town to ask and we picked the local idiot." Pat eased back into the thin flow of traffic.

" I'm nearly sure those are the lights where I saw Tony the Terrible. I wasn't expecting to be down here again so soon." Brenda laughed to herself at the silliness of it.

They had slept late, very late, and had shuffled about while Pat made 'brunch for the living dead'. The drive down to Stanton had been uninterrupted except when Pat had to stop at a McDonalds for a 'McPee'. Both were surprised their hangovers weren't worse, but they were quiet on the journey and the excitement they were expecting had yet to kick in.

At about the same time as they pulled away from the kerb Ross Walker, to the ribbing of his companions, missed an easy putt at the sixteenth.

They found Treadle Avenue independent of the man's directions. The area seemed in decline, the houses just a degree or so away from shabbiness.

"Well, this is it, the Taylor demesne. Any nerves?"

"Nerves?" asked Pat, and her voice sounded too loud to her. "Why should I be nervous? You're the one who's going to do the business. I'm strictly an observer. Bit grubby, isn't it?"

"Slow down a bit. 18, 20, 22, 24, 26 – that's it, 28, with the blue door and the FOR SALE sign. Look at those awful net curtains. Don't stop, don't stop, drive on down and we'll turn and park down a bit on his side where he can't see us."

Pat did as instructed. They could see the front edge of the house, the patch of lawn and the Agent's sign, but the angle was too oblique to see the windows or door.

Pat broke the little silence that had descended when she had switched off the engine. "Just look at the two of us sitting here like a pair of fourth formers."

"And why not? Why should fourth formers have all the fun?"

Pat was beginning to feel the delayed effects of the previous evening's drinking; an unpleasant heat settled on her and she felt a little sweat on her brow. "Knowing my luck, he's not in," she said, not sure what her feelings were.

"Knowing your luck he's sitting in there by himself hoping for somebody to take to see *Halloween 11* or *12* or whatever."

Pat managed a smile, but the place was depressing. "Sir Anthony doesn't seem to have done too well for himself. I think I'm glad our big romance didn't blossom."

"You're probably right, but you never can tell. Some of these old houses can be— what's the jargon – 'very desirable residences'."

"Either that, or he's got a big place in the country, and this is just his secret love nest for a bit of cheap on the sly. Wonder why it's up for sale?"

Brenda was studying what she could see of the house. "Don't see any swing or toys or evidence of young heirs to the estate. I'm going to have a look. He won't recognise me. I'll ask for directions or a kiss or something. I just want a look." She broke into song as she unhooked her seatbelt:

Just one look, that's all it took,

Yeah, just one look."

"You're a nutcase, d'you know that?" Pat's voice had none of the lightness she intended.

Brenda was out of the car. She leaned in to Pat. "D'you think he'll ask me in? If I'm not back in ten minutes, send in the cavalry or a SWAT team or something... You're supposed to say 'Come back, you brave fool' at this point."

Suddenly Pat's mouth was dry and nervousness flooded through her, leaving a tingling that made her almost numb. "Brenda, let's just go home. I've got a bad feeling about this. Please don't go into the house. I really hope he isn't in."

But Brenda wasn't listening. "It is a far, far better thing that I do than I have ever done," and the car door closed and she was striding towards the house, her shoulder bag swaying with each step.

Ross swung the bag of clubs on to his shoulder at the eighteenth, the first round completed, him in the lead, and the prospect of a drink at the clubhouse lengthening the stride of all four golfers.

Pat watched what was happening like a spectator with no control over the game.

Brenda walked up to the house, waved back to her, knocked, and waited. Then she was in conversation with someone, but whoever it was stayed inside and Pat couldn't see him. Next thing Brenda gave a comic little circular wave in Pat's direction and disappeared into the house. Pat discovered she had been holding her breath.

"She's in, the nutter. I knew she would, I knew it," she said aloud, to break the tension, a mixture of uneasiness and curiosity swirling in her head. Would Brenda run riot now and reveal who she was, and tell Tony that she was waiting outside in the car? Part of her cringed, another part hoped...

It seemed to Pat that twenty minutes had gone, she couldn't be sure, and there was no sign at all of Brenda. She found herself repeating over and over, "Where is she?" and "What's keeping her?" the irritation in her voice quickly giving way to anxiety and then to real fear as Brenda's words echoed round in her mind: *Taylor was always a bit weird. He's scarier than the film. I'm surprised he didn't bite you in the neck.* Pat found her hands were actually shaking and there was a coldness in her stomach that had nothing to do with a hangover. If only she knew what was happening, if Brenda was safe. Suddenly she thought of the mobile in Brenda's bag. Her mind raced so hard it couldn't get hold of Brenda's number, but she forced herself to calm down, and remembered it was one of the stored numbers on her own mobile's address book.

"Please answer, please answer," she begged aloud as the number rang; *I'm sorry, the person you have called is not available. Please leave your message after the tone.* Not available. Why? Where was she? What had happened to her? There was no time to look for help, no other way, she had to go to Taylor's door and find out by herself...

They had decided after a couple of drinks to have a leisurely lunch in the clubhouse restaurant and give themselves time for an easygoing second round in the afternoon. Ross studied the menu; he always ate fairly lightly when he was playing golf.

The open door unnerved her. It had swung open when she raised the rusty knocker on the faded blue top panel. Her first tentative 'Hello' told her instantly that the house was empty; the sound echoed down the dark hall and in the bare rooms, scaring her by its aloneness. She wanted to turn and run back outside, but concern for her good, true friend was stronger than even the terror that made her heart hammer and her legs weak. She moved deeper in, towards the centre of the house.

Pat was calling for her friend, calling her name, Brenda, Brenda, when a gun came out of the semi-darkness and shot her at point blank range through the temple. The flash lit up for a second the gun, wrapped in a nightdress, as it smoked in Brenda's hands, and its muffled boom thumped in the heart of the desolate house.

The noise reverberated in Brenda's head long after the house was again silent. She still held the gun with both hands, arms out straight in front as Ross had shown her. *Walk away when it's done,* he had told her, *don't look at her,* but she couldn't stop herself looking down. Pat's body lay against her feet, the face white in the gloom, a stream of blood moving slowly away from the head.

Brenda shivered and dragged her eyes away. She shuddered as she stepped over the body and sat on the bottom wooden stair. Her mind desperately tried to recall Ross's last words. They were in her bed, their bodies warm and exhausted: *Once it's done you must stay calm. It won't be easy, but think of me, of us, and you can do it. When this is all over we'll be free. Take some of the brandy and you'll be OK until I come for you. You'll have to wait until after dark, but you can do it, you can do it. I love you, Brenda darling, you know I love you.*

Ross finished his drink, lit a cigarette, and motioned to the barman to repeat the round. The hotel bar was full with its Saturday evening regulars; Ross's group had finished their meal early to secure their favourite spot at the end of the long gleaming bar counter.

The street lighting was poor, but there was just enough light in the hallway to pick out the two pale faces on the floor, both surprised in death; a mess of blood had leaked from one of them, while near the other something had spilled from a hip flask on the floor and had trickled into the darkness.

KEY ISSUE

Matt took his time over breakfast. It was his favourite meal of the day. He loved the early morning smells: hot milk on cornflakes, burnt toast, grilled bacon. They reminded him of hotels and holidays. And then that first cup of tea, so hot that he could feel a light sweat on his forehead. His workmates marvelled how he could drink his tea scalding hot, while they had to blow into their mugs, or wait till their tea cooled. They joked that his mouth must be asbestos lined.

"You must have that asbestosis thing they're always warnin' us about," and Matt joined in the laughter.

His workmates. The word pleased Matt. He liked being one of a team, the belonging, the banter. There had been none of that in his two previous jobs. Here each man had his part to play, his job to do, each respected the others' importance to the success of the unit. There were only four of them, but that made his feeling of responsibility greater and more satisfying. As the youngest, and the most recent, he might have experienced the distance or unfriendliness that often faced the new arrival, but he had found none of that from any of the other three.

Matt allowed himself the luxury of a second cup of tea, put his lunchbox and flask into the canvas bag, and left the breakfast dishes on the table. He'd do them later. On his way down to the truck he nipped in as usual to the corner shop for his daily provisions: cigarettes, chewing gum, and The Sun to give him his opinions for the day. It was one of those sharpish September mornings with that distinctive back-to-school feel in the air. How he had hated school. He could still feel a fluttery stomach on mornings like this. Now, however, he had the fresh mint taste of gum in his mouth, his packet of ciggies, and his morning paper. Great.

Matt was proud of always being first on site, already having a smoke by the time his mates arrived. He walked briskly down to the scrap of waste ground at the foot of the street where the truck was parked, rubbing his hands together in the satisfaction of being young, of belonging.

The trouble presented itself at first as a minor inconvenience, a nuisance. He couldn't find the key for the truck. He must have left it on the kitchen table. Before trotting back to the flat, Matt searched through his pockets several more times, because the key was normally in his jeans pocket and he didn't remember seeing it at breakfast. It wasn't there, it definitely wasn't on his person.

It wasn't in the flat either. He was sure of that, because he had turned the place upside down. He had even searched in silly places, like the cornflakes packet and the grill pan, and totally daft places, like inside his guitar and inside his football boots in the zippered sports bag. Nothing. Another dive into his pockets, and a glance at the watch. Still time to find the key and get there to meet his mates and pick up the load of tiles for the job. Where could it be? What could he have done with it? If only he had had a duplicate.

Think it out. He had locked the truck the previous evening, come home, and hadn't been out. Nor had anyone been in who might have lifted it. Could he have dropped it in the street, or in the shop? A thorough search. Negative again. Suddenly a little two-inch piece of metal was the most important thing in his life, upsetting his happiness, threatening his world. Another desperate, fruitless search of his pockets. They'd be at the site by now, waiting for him. Matt felt his heart thumping and his face redden in pure frustration.

Maybe he had dropped it in the street after all, probably the previous evening, and it had been picked up. O.K., forget about looking for the key and instead look for other solutions. If he could get inside the cab, he'd soon get her started. He'd hot-wired enough vehicles back in his joyriding days, before he'd 'turned the corner', as his probation officer had put it. The rear window was the obvious way to cause least damage, but he hesitated. He was still paying off the truck to his brother-in-law Terry, who had proved right in promising that it would make him more independent and help him get employment. Matt didn't doubt that it was the truck that had clinched his present job.

He ran back again to the flat for a broad screwdriver, climbed into the back of his truck, and tried to ease out the glass. Useless. The glass seemed to be imbedded into the rubber, and allowed the screwdriver no purchase at all. He dug in deeply with the point of the screwdriver to get underneath the pane, but the only result of his efforts was a badly gouged window surround.

What now? Don't panic. A key would solve everything, but what key, and where would he get it? Answer: the garage that supplied the truck in the first place. With the hope that comes with a course of action, Matt got change from the shop and ran up to the phone box to ring his sister. For a moment he feared it would be vandalised or out of order, so the dialling tone came as a relief. There was no phone book, of course, but he knew the number. Would Marlene be in? She was, and Matt quickly outlined the quandary he was in. She arranged to get in touch with her husband, find out where he had bought the truck, and pick Matt up to purchase a replacement key…

"Basically we can only supply a set of keys with a vehicle, basically. We don't basically keep keys, and we don't basically cut extra keys. What we can basically do, sir, is give you the number of the key you basically need, and the address of the Agency that basically supplies them." The girl checked her nail varnish.

Matt had dropped Marlene off at her house and driven the ten miles in her car to the garage, only to learn now what he could have been told by phone. The journey had been 'basically' a waste of time. The girl punched the details of Matt's truck into her computer, patted her lipstick with a tissue, and handed him a printout of the key number.

Matt drove in a simmering rage the fifteen miles to the main Datsun Agency and got three keys cut. On the way back he felt obliged to put £10 of petrol into the car. The phrase 'costly mistake' he read regularly on The Sun's Sports page was taking on a very real meaning.

It was now well after ten o'clock. They would be wondering what had happened to him to hold up the day's work. Should he go to the site first and tell them what was going on? No, what good would that do; better to arrive later and have the tiles with him. If only he had some way of getting in touch, if only somebody could invent a phone that people could carry about with them…

They didn't fit. The new keys wouldn't fit. He couldn't believe it, but none of the keys would fit either door. A sweat of desperation broke on Matt's brow, and he cursed the keys, the truck, the girl, the Agency, himself, with every swear word his nineteen years could muster. But wait a bit. Maybe they would fit the ignition? His own key had fitted both the doors and the ignition, but maybe somehow the new ones were only for starting. He had to get in to find out.

He was tempted to smash the window in, but the likely mess and expense ruled it out. He studied the door. The inside handle was near the front. If he were to cut a small aperture on the outside of the door, he might be able to locate the handle rodding and turn the lock. Once more he ran back to the flat, and returned with his toolbox. There was no implement that recommended itself for the job, so Matt chose a hammer and four-inch nail and carefully punched a circle of holes through the panel. He was surprised how easily the metal was penetrated. When the perforated circle was complete, Matt lined up his screwdriver and whacked it with the hammer. The metal circle obligingly gave way, dropped down inside the door panel, and revealed…another panel.

This one was a couple of inches further inside. There was no sign of the handle mechanism. The plan was a failure, he was back to square one…

Matt closed his eyes and swung the hammer, expecting it to bounce back, but the glass fractured first time into a large sagging mosaic handkerchief. He was able to coax most of it outside and let it fall on the ground, so the mess in the footwell wasn't nearly so bad as he had feared. Matt reached inside, released the lock, and he was in.

How had he been stupid enough, even for a minute, to think that the keys would fit the ignition? Of course they didn't, not one of them.

Why was everything going wrong? How could he be back where he started, on his own, with nobody to help him? Matt lit a cigarette for comfort and saw that his fingers were shaking, in rage, frustration, helplessness. Part of him wanted to pack the whole thing in, to go back to the sanctuary of the flat, curl up on the bed, and listen to his tapes, but the better side of him knew he couldn't do that. He threw the cigarette end out the vacant window and set to work on the plastic shrouding round the steering wheel. Eventually he manoeuvred the lock system off the steering column, and tried bridging the wires. Sparks spat at him, and the wiring loom glowed like a toaster, but although the engine turned over several times it wasn't prepared to start. From somewhere Matt managed to dredge up a few additional swear words to add to the impressive recital he had given earlier.

As he sat biting his fingernails, a habit he thought he had conquered at primary school, Matt noticed a number on the ignition lock barrel dangling down among the rat's nest of wires. It looked familiar. He checked it against the keys he had had cut. They matched exactly apart from the final number, which was a 7 on the barrel and a 1 on the keys.

That was it. The stupid bitch had got her make-up right and his number wrong. Had she been present at that moment, Matt's hammer would have found further employment...

He rang the Datsun Agency from the phone box and they confirmed, after a long wait and four more 10p pieces into the slot, that he had the wrong keys. Matt drove the 14 miles back to the Agency and got three new keys cut. The man behind the counter listened sympathetically to Matt's misfortunes before charging him the full price for all three keys. Matt felt older, and was definitely poorer, when he called back for his sister and drove back with her to the truck. He expected the broken window to have inspired further vandalism in his absence, but, with the schools restarted, this fear proved unfounded.

Marlene waited to see if the new key fitted. It did, smoothly. She was just about to drive off when the 'bomb' went off. Matt had turned the key in the ignition to start the truck when he heard and felt the loud explosion below him. He jumped out, soothed his sister, who was checking herself for injuries, and looked underneath the back of his truck. The silencer and part of the exhaust pipe had split completely open, like a banana skin. Matt laughed. It was the irrational laugh of the broken man. He got back in the truck and started it up. It sounded like a pneumatic drill with asthma.

The tiles got through. At a steady 15 m.p.h., and fearing police interest all the way, Matt had driven the 5 miles to pick them up. He arrived at the site in time to find the men starting their lunch. They came out to see what was making the din, and Matt hurried an explanation. As they unloaded the tiles Matt repeated, in full detail, everything that had happened. He wasn't sure whether to expect sympathy, admiration, or condemnation, but they said little and at the end seemed more interested in their sandwich fillings. Matt then realised that in the crisis he had left his canvas bag in his sister's car, and had no lunch with him.

"You go and get yourself somethin' to eat. There's that wee shop two streets down on the corner."

Wasn't that just typical of them - he'd kept them waiting all morning, and, instead of blaming him, they were concerned about his lunch. Matt felt a glow of gratitude. He thought of the torrent of abuse he would have got from the so-called mates he had got mixed up with in the old days.

He had gone just a few yards when he nearly tripped over a loose shoelace. As he stooped to tie it he felt something digging into his thigh. He checked. There it was, in a needless, useless tiny extra pocket inside the top of the main pocket of his jeans, the little piece of metal that had ruined his day, the key to all his torment.

Matt had to smile, in spite of all that had happened. His mates would get a great laugh when they heard this. He imagined the good-natured ribbing, and turned back right away to start the joke rolling.

They were settling down on a plank bench to finish devouring their packed lunches and didn't hear him approaching the open doorway.

"I told you from the start he was a waste of space."

"Aye, and a shirt lifter too, if you ask me. D'ye ever see the way he goes on past the Page 3 girls? I never trust a man who shows no interest in a woman's bumpers."

"Never mind the bumpers, he's costin' us time and money. We coulda got them tiles delivered free, no matter about his bloody truck. We'll give him till the weekend and get rid of him."

"We could always take him on as tea boy."

"Tea boy? Are you serious? He'd blister the gobs off us."

The sniggers were ringing in Matt's head as he slipped over to the truck, wondering how fast he could get away, how much noise he would make, how much the repairs would cost, and if there was any chance Terry might take the truck back again…

GAME PLAN

She'd never agree to murder. Irene hated Morrow just as much as he did, perhaps even more, but she'd never agree to killing him. James was certain of it. He had tested her once after one of her daily outbursts.

"He's ruined our lives, James, Morrow has ruined our lives, and here we sit doing nothing about it. There must be something we can do, there has to be something. Our lives are a nightmare."

"Getting rid of the body's always the problem," he joked experimentally.

She glared at him. "Don't be stupid, James. I'm serious. We can't go on like this."

Just like a woman: Irene would pile up a mountain of affronts and grievances, plead for an answer to them, and then dismiss the best and only solution.

She was right to an extent, though. In many ways he was stupid. It was stupid, for example, to go on blaming their former neighbour Ingram for starting all their troubles, but if only the mousy little accountant next door hadn't been fiddling figures and taking backhanders from his high profile clients, or at least if he had not been caught. The case had made the front pages for a day or two: Ingram had been given a two year suspended sentence, had had to put the house on the market to meet fines and legal costs, and Irene and he had suffered the punishment ever since.

Yes, they were the ones paying the penalty for the crime. It came in the form of their new neighbour, their tormentor, their scourge, Todd Morrow. James recalled his first sighting of the man who had totally wrecked their contented existence. The removal van was offloading its contents and as James watched from behind a curtain he assumed that the man shouting instructions and threats to the other two was their boss. It was a real surprise later that evening when he answered the knock at the door, saw the 'removal man' with his hand extended, and heard him pronouncing the life sentence: "Hello, I'm Todd Morrow. I'm your new neighbour."

Next thing, the man was in the lounge, talking non-stop, mostly about himself, lifting Irene's best ornaments and checking their base, exploring the downstairs rooms. Irene and he found themselves trooping along behind, as their guide led them through their own house. He was like a tornado. The best they could do was watch for breakages, as they did every time Irene's sister arrived with her two dreadful children. Their 'guest' was in full flow.

"Looking back, I find it hard to believe myself how fast it all happened. Yes, started with just one car, done her up myself, sold her on and bought two more, and look at me now."

They looked and hated, instantly and permanently. Morrow was in his thirties, well built and with fairish hair permed in tight curls. Irene was sure afterwards that his tan was real, in spite of her husband's hope that it had come bottled. One ear was studded, bolder jewellery encircled fingers and wrists. The open red shirt showed a medallion nestling in a hairy chest. His aftershave seemed to permeate the house like disinfectant. The business success story was building:

"Then came the famous day when the manager was off sick, and they put me in charge till he came back. Management - I got a taste of it, and I liked it. From that day on I knew I was going to be boss of my own business. Let me tell you this, I had to learn fast, and I expect my staff to learn fast too. Ask me once, no problem. Ask me a second time, well, O.K. Ask me a third time.... oh brother!!"

As Morrow laughed at the fate awaiting a slow learner, James got an opening to offer him a drink.

"Thought you'd never ask. Used to be a pint man, but a man's tastes change as his fortunes change, as my old man used to say. Can still put away a pint with the best of them, mind, but nowadays it's the old G and T for yours truly."

They were shell-shocked by the man's crassness and familiarity. "This here's what put me where I am today," tapping his head. "The slogan did the business: *BUY THE CAR OFF T. MORROW* – get it? Nice one, eh, love? I was always good at gimmicks and stunts and the like."

Later: "So, just the two of you, no son and heir. No lead in the old pencil, Jimmy?" Still later: "Bit of luck for me Ingram getting caught out. I got the house at the right price, cash up front. I knew the guy needed it right away. Cars, houses, it's all the same to me. Know your man, know your money, that's my motto. Must have been a surprise to the neighbours, him being involved in a scam like that. Different if it had been the like of you or me, eh, Jimmy?" Laugh and wink.

Morrow kept on refilling his glass and splashing in tonic, while his hosts sat nervously sipping theirs. When he finally left, with darkness starting to settle, James found himself making a mental note to add gin to the weekly shopping list.

"Tell me it's not true, James, tell me I've been having a bad dream. Tell me that creature isn't real, that he's not really going to live in Grangeview Court, that he doesn't intend to settle next door to us."

Irene was slumped on the couch, exhausted. James took her hand and in a thin voice told her all the things he hoped were true, and knew in his heart were not. "It'll be all right, Irene, it'll be all right. He won't stay. It'll be too quiet for him here. Anyhow, he can't be that obnoxious all the time. We've just seen the worst of him, that's all."

Grangeview Court was a long curving avenue where, for once, the developers had shown sensitivity and good sense. It had formerly been the drive of an eighteenth century mansion. The original ancient firs and pines that had bordered the drive had been carefully landscaped into the individual gardens of the development to complement the Georgian style dwellings. The sweep of the avenue was such that the two houses at the top, those of James and Irene, and Todd Morrow, were slightly removed from the others, and partitioned from them to some extent by the alignment of the trees. As a result, they were seen as the most private and exclusive. Another consequence of the geography was that the other residents were unaffected by the arrival of Morrow into their neighbourhood, and largely unaware of the activities that soon began to blight the lives of James and Irene.

The trouble started almost immediately. James was having breakfast a few mornings after Morrow's self-introduction when he heard a loud buzzing outside, followed by a shriek from the kitchen. Irene came rushing in, her face white.
"He's cutting down our hedge, James, he's cutting down our hedge."
James rushed out, scattering toast crumbs from his napkin, and sure enough, there was Morrow busily barbering their precious beech hedge with a chainsaw.
"What do you think you're doing?" James spluttered. "That's our hedge."
Morrow heard him at the third splutter and allowed the saw to idle for a moment. "What do I think I'm doing? I know what I'm doing, old son. This is a march hedge, and by law I can cut it down if it's causing a nuisance. Well, it's cutting the light out of my back patio, so I'm entitled to take it down a bit. I know the law, my son. You have to, in my line of business."
Then he was addressing the hedge again with the chainsaw, and James found himself trailing back inside with his mouth hanging open.
That was the first of a series of brushes James had with Morrow, and in every one, whether it concerned sheds, fences, parking or boundary lines, he came out a very poor second. They all ended the same way, with a humiliated James sitting afterwards thinking of the things he should have said or should have done. The business of the weedkiller was a case in point. Morrow had been spraying weeds at the side of the house and enough of it had blown over to wither a bed of Irene's roses,

and leave several large freckles on the back lawn.

"One of those things," said Morrow, when James bowed to his wife's pressure and confronted him. "Nobody's fault. It's what's called an Act of God. In law the wind would be an Act of God, so nobody would be held responsible. These things happen, old son. Nothing to do with me."

What could the mild-mannered James do in the face of a bulldozer like Todd Morrow? Every day Irene and he came home from work dreading what lay at the top of the avenue. The front lawn of *Dunroamin*, as the house was now called, was populated by B&Q gnomes clustered near a PVC gazebo. Coloured light bulbs were strung round the house and garden, their illumination assisted by plastic Victorian gaslamps and a reproduction coach lamp at each side of the door.

All this, of course, was a mere sideshow. James and Irene could have lived fairly readily with Morrow's tastelessness, perhaps even derived some fun from it, but it was the man's antics, activities, lifestyle, whatever name best described the goings-on, that were destroying their peace and threatening their sanity.

How naïve they were to regard the first party as a one-off, a housewarming do where excesses could be expected as part of the celebration. Irene was sufficiently relaxed to try a joke. "Maybe they're celebrating Morrow living somewhere else, well away from them."

The guests started arriving about seven. James was in the front garden, expurgating dandelions with a kitchen fork, and could hear the music of clinking bottles that conducted them from their cars to the front door. Cigarette smoke and perfume drifted across in the mild autumn air, and giggles and high heel clickings reached him over his sweet escalonia hedge. Morrow, in polo shirt and biting on a slim cigar, was feinting punches at the men and clutching the women. James caught himself watching the women. They had their hair piled high, deep cleavages, long legs, and wore very heavy make-up, short dresses and impossibly high heels, giving overall an appearance not unlike the saucy blonde barmaids and naughty nurses of the seaside postcard. James swallowed hard and went into the house...

"Thank goodness that's over. My nerves couldn't take much more." Irene's head sank back into the pillow. The doors of the last car had slammed, its lights swung across their bedroom wall. Lying with eyes open and bodies tense, they had listened until almost four in the morning the thumping music and drunken squeals, laughter and shouting that were to become the signature tune of the parties next door. The pattern was set.

When midnight arrived the next weekend with another riotous party in full swing,

James took a deep breath and marched across to a house lit up like a Mississippi riverboat. He was met at the door by a pneumatic blonde who, assuring him that things were just starting to warm up, instructed him to leave his drink in the bar on the left.

James eventually located Morrow in the kitchen, and heard him promising a couple of excited young women that he'd have the swimming pool ready before the end of the year. He spotted James. "Come on in, old son. What's your poison?"

When he learned through the tobacco smoke that James was there to complain about the noise, his tone changed. "A moment, friend. Nobody's causing any bother here, nobody but yourself. You'll need to learn to live and let live, my son. That's my motto, live and let live. You go ahead and have as many parties as you want, and it won't bother me. No, you'll get no complaints from me." He drained his glass to affirm the promise.

James returned home wondering what version of the meeting would distress his wife least. He noticed for the first time how quiet their house was, like a public library. Some little rebel part deep inside whispered that it preferred the perfumed noise and movement next door, but he squashed the insurgent thought in an instant.

As the noise and nuisance of Morrow's parties continued, they called the police, of course, but even as Irene was starting her lament to the policeman and WPC who called, James knew it was a lost cause.

He saw the woman constable take in the domestic order of the room, the little dusted glass ornaments, the magazines in a rack, the gleaming furniture, and exchange a smile with her colleague. James too smiled, in spite of himself. He was remembering the Christmas his father had stayed over, and had thrown on the fire the group of small varnished logs that Irene had arranged so artistically on the hearth.

The policeman was speaking to him. "We'll have a word with Mr. Morrow, sir, and make sure he turns the volume down, so to speak. Maybe you can keep an eye on things..."

How could they do otherwise, when Morrow was keeping a dozen or more of his used cars at the front, and his visitors were repeatedly parking on their lawn, blocking their driveway, littering the area. James felt like a solitary fireman trying to fight a forest inferno.

The men were all as obnoxious as their host, it seemed, and had the same disagreeable habits, such as addressing James as 'squire' or 'sport' when he protested about their behaviour. One morning about two o'clock, with a party at its height, James saw three of them urinating on his lawn. He prevented Irene from watching and, still fully dressed, marched downstairs and outside.

"Would you mind not doing that," he called out in the sternest voice he could muster.

"Keep your hair on, chief. This'll make the grass grow quicker," and they sniggered loudly. James felt his bald head glow in helpless rage.

As for the women, they were another matter. In a different way they caused James greater disquiet. Irene and he had agreed early in the Morrow tyranny that they would stand firm together, not allow themselves to take out their frustrations upon each other, and never move house. If anything good could be said to have come from the arrival of the neighbour from hell, it was that husband and wife presented a wholly united front, suffering bravely together under the same persecution.

Then James found himself watching the 'sluts' in secret, with a dry mouth and hollow tummy, sneaking looks, strange desires stirring, whether half remembered or half forgotten he wasn't sure. Afterwards terrible feelings of guilt and shame would assail him: where Irene felt nothing but outrage and dismay, he was poaching little private satisfactions and sensations. There were nights when James lay sleepless as a traitor.

The strength of her resolve served to sharpen these stabs of guilt. One day when Morrow had lit a fire in his garden and the black smoke had blown straight into her washing, an extraordinary thing happened. Irene used the F word. James had never heard her swear before. He admired her defiance and resistance, but a little part of him was saddened: Morrow's coarseness was like a plague, affecting everything in its path, including the finest flowers.

James was starting to have other feelings too, feelings even more disturbing than those aroused by the females on the guest list next door. They started with fairly infantile fancies: smashing all Morrow's windows, slashing his tyres, spraying graffiti on his walls, the usual imaginings of a bully's victim. These revenge fancies, however, began to deepen into something darker, heavier. At first the violence was in the form of disturbed dreams, in which James saw himself, or felt himself, inflicting horrifying injuries on people he didn't recognise, often using sledgehammers or axes or iron bars. At no time in these dreams was Morrow the one on the receiving end of the terrible blows. James would awake instantly from the nightmares, breathless, his heart thumping, the nerves in his stomach churning. He said nothing to Irene about them, but the dreams were so unlike anything he had ever experienced before that they affected him greatly, making him anxious and nervy.

Then the thoughts started: appalling thoughts, thoughts of sadistic torture and killing, thoughts that the meek James would never have believed himself capable of conceiving.

He thought of kidnapping Morrow, chaining him to a wall in some remote building, and watching him die in agony from starvation; he sat gorging delicious meals as his captive begged for a scrap of food. Some of the thoughts and imaginings were so barbarous that he had to drag his mind to other things to avoid facing them. Yet they kept coming back – Morrow hanging by his feet as James blinded him in each eye; Morrow tied up and helpless as James doused him in petrol and lit the match... What was happening to him? Was he going mad? He dared not share these frightful pictures with Irene: in spite of his best intentions, the bond between them was loosening.

The solution to everything was clearer by the day: he would have to get rid of the source of all their troubles, Todd Morrow, and he would have to do it by himself. It was just a matter of how...

The programme was one of those needless pre-match analysis pieces, the expert in the studio bland and infallible, but for James his words had the authority of an Instruction Manual: *They're the weaker side and they'll be on the back foot throughout the 90 minutes. Their only hope is to play to whatever strengths they have, sit tight at the back, and hope the other team gets careless. In every match there's always a half chance, a gap that a quick break from defence might be able to exploit. Who knows, they might even sneak a result.*

James waited until Irene had gone to bed, got a sheet of A4 paper, and ruled a line down its middle. He headed the left side MY STRENGTHS and the right MORROW'S WEAKNESSES. The sides balanced better than he dared to hope. In his favour, apart from the motivating force of total hatred for the enemy and determination to destroy him, were two key elements. First, his job. As Distribution Manager of Pharmacom, the largest pharmaceutical company in the county, he had unhindered access to virtually every drug and chemical substance in the book. The second factor was equally advantageous: he had direct entry into Morrow's house.

Morrow himself always drove into the garage through the electronically controlled door and entered the house by the inside door, but on a number of occasions, from behind his curtain, James had seen employees let themselves into the house through the back door, using a key they took from a shelf in the greenhouse. They always returned the key when their errand was over.

As James underlined, and then circled, these two vital strengths, a kind of excitement was building in him, the excitement of criminal secrecy. It was a feeling new to him, and he was surprised by its power. When he glanced across the page the excitement increased. Written there, and underlined, were the words *Routine* and *Habits*. Were these weaknesses, openings to be exploited? In the early days, before the cold war had set in, Morrow would confide to James his success formula, confident that it would be found interesting. One of his practices was of particular interest now. He kept his Used Car Showroom open late two nights a week, Tuesdays and Thursdays.

"Work hard, and play hard, but don't mix the two. That's my motto, old son, and I haven't done too bad by it. A couple of snifters from Mr Gordon when I come in on the late nights, a little bit of the old TV, and I'm into the straw. Even the top stud needs an early night or two to recharge the batteries."

Thursday. James added the word to the other two and drew a box round it. Thursday, the evening Irene went to her Italian class. He dropped her off each week at the college before half seven and was home again in ten minutes. A woman from the class left her at the bottom of the avenue, and she got back about ten. Morrow got home round half eight. Plenty of time. James felt a nervous satisfaction as the thing started to take shape. He gave a kind of laugh, and instantly looked over his shoulder. Was this really happening? Was he, all by himself, in his own armchair and surrounded by everyday familiar things, sitting planning murder...

The best laid plans...the mission was almost aborted before it got off the ground. Irene's gold bracelet somehow came apart just as they were leaving the house, and by the time he had found the small pliers and mended the fault, they were running late. His hands trembled as he did the repair.

"Never mind, James, it doesn't matter. I'll just miss the class this week. Don't get into a state over it."

He dropped her off, but the anxiety stayed with him as he drove back. Should he go ahead as planned, or was the delay an omen? Strangely, once he got into the plan itself, as he had rehearsed it again and again in his mind over the past few weeks, his nerves steadied and he was back in control. First he phoned Morrow's house, prefacing the number by 141, to confirm there was nobody home. Then he slipped out the side door and slid through the gap in the hedge into Morrow's back garden.

For a moment he worried that the greenhouse door might perversely be locked, but it lay open as usual and his surgical-gloved hand found the key immediately. Everything now depended on the back door of the house having no interior lock or bolt.... the key turned smoothly, the door pushed open, and he was in Morrow's house.

Every house has its smell. This one was a blend of pub, cinema, and Indian restaurant. James stood breathless, motionless, listening to the hammering of his heart. He counted to ten, and then made his way softly into the room with the massive television screen in the corner, facing Morrow's wide leather armchair. James gave a sigh of relief. On the small table beside the chair was a bottle of Gordons, half full, attended by a plastic Family Size bottle of tonic. His heart raced, but his hands were remarkably steady as he took a phial from his inside pocket and poured its contents equally into both bottles.

The Strychlometoxamen 22, according to its report, was lethal, instant, virtually undetectable, producing the symptoms of occlusion of coronary artery leading to myocardial infarction. In less than a minute the back door was relocked and James was in his own garden, walking just a little too quickly.

The big fear was that Morrow might have other plans that evening or, worse still, would arrive home with a colleague or woman friend. James's plan was predicated on his belief in the man's vanity. Morrow felt that everything he did was right, perfect, and, in the interest of continuing success, routines were not to be altered. When his car rounded the curve just after half past eight, and he the sole occupant, James sagged with relief. He had unconsciously been holding his breath. He watched the car enter the garage and the automatic door close.

This was the worst part. What if Morrow decided not to have a drink, or chose something other than gin? But no, he'd said it himself, he was a G and T man. James paced up and down, up and down, afraid of the phone ringing, the doorbell ringing, afraid even to look out the window. How long should he wait? Might Irene arrive back early? Was the Strychlometoxamen as effective as its dossier claimed?

He kept putting back the deadline to make the call, but at a quarter to ten he knew he dared wait no longer. With dry mouth and pounding head, he pressed Redial, finger poised to cut off the call should it be answered.

Nothing. No reply. James let the ringing continue for a minute. He had to be sure, before returning to get the bottles and whatever glass or glasses Morrow might have used. He'd kept the key and would replace it on the way back.

The house was totally silent inside. Why was the TV not on? Did Morrow somehow suspect something, was he hiding, waiting to spring out? Had he perhaps gone straight to the gin bottle? James tiptoed towards the room, his temples surely going to explode. He stopped outside the open door, needing to look, afraid to look, then took a deep breath and stepped inside the doorway.

James's knees went weak, his heart stopped. The armchair was empty, the room unoccupied. As his mind reeled and he sensed that Morrow was standing right behind him, he suddenly realised that the table was bare, the two bottles missing. In an instant all was clear. Morrow had gone to bed and taken his nightcap with him.

The thick carpet made no sound under his feet. The master bedroom was the second on the landing, its door half open. James listened outside for a moment, eyes closed in fear and concentration, but there was no sound of breathing. Suddenly he took two paces inside and opened his eyes.

Morrow lay naked on the bed, his mouth drooling, his eyes wide in death. Across him was slumped the naked body of a woman. James did not need to see the face. The dead hand clutching at Morrow's chest had a bracelet on its wrist, with a mended link in its gold chain.

OPENING BID

It seemed to Mervyn that the Auction Room was even busier than it normally was the last Saturday afternoon of each month. By now he could identify not just a number of individuals, but also the behaviour patterns of various dealers and bidders who flooded the large high-ceilinged room with its sweating walls and dusty doorframes. He enjoyed watching anxious punters standing over the objects of their desire, as if in so doing they could protect them from the interest or observation of others.

Mervyn rarely put in a bid for an item: he kept in mind one of his father's many pet sayings: *a bargain's not a bargain if it's something you don't need.* In any case, whether he needed it or not, his mother was sure to condemn any purchase as something that would need dusting, along with everything else in the house. He sometimes pictured her standing in perfect happiness in a house cleared of all furniture, furnishings and fittings, her private dust-free paradise.

As he made his way down one of the cluttered aisles Mervyn suddenly found himself staring at the face and features that had tormented him virtually all of his 27 years. They stared back out of a worn gilt-framed mirror, that unmistakable huge horn nose and the spectacular pair of jug handle ears, booby prizes awarded to him on a non-returnable basis by a cruel nature. Mervyn felt yet again, as he had done every day since a young child first able to understand the hurtfulness of others, the unfairness of things.

The teasing he had suffered at school was merely the start of a life sentence delivered upon a wholly innocent victim. Mervyn had soon come to expect, if never accept, the traditional nicknames, the Beaky and Dumbo variety that attached all through his school career. It was when he started as an apprentice in the aircraft factory that the more technical ones had begun: *Dive Brakes and Wingflaps* were two that stuck.

Many of the men didn't even know his real name: "Are you goin' to the meetin' this Friday, Wingflaps?" or "Did you hear, Concorde, they're cuttin' down on all weekend overtime?" They had just assumed he wouldn't take offence. Even his workmate and friend Jimmy, Jimmy the joker, used to throw out one-liners like 'I wish I had been born rich instead of good-looking', making no allowance for Mervyn's sensibilities.

If one positive had been gained from the injustice of Mervyn's appearance, it was this: he could never be insensitive to the feelings of other people, never exploit others' misfortune. In his blackest moments, however, Mervyn hated his parents, his father for having passed on to him in exaggerated form his own worst features, and his mother for not having had his ears corrected as a toddler, as others had done, by simple surgery.

He had once mentioned to gruff old Dr Byers the idea of cosmetic surgery, and had been given a dampening reply: "Nonsense. Aren't you in perfect health? Time enough looking for surgery when you need it." Later, when Byers had retired, his place was taken by a young lady doctor, but Mervyn was too embarrassed to pursue the matter. In some ways he was relieved to have her as an excuse.

Mervyn pushed through the crowd, distantly noting the familiar smell of stale clothes, old wood and mouldy plaster, the body odour of the room. Sunk in his own bitter thoughts he hardly noticed that the business itself had started at the front of the room; the little auctioneer in the stained green waistcoat was already on Lot 4.

Mervyn marvelled how his audience could laugh at the same patter they heard regularly, once a month – "Who's going to start me at five hundred pound, who's going to come in at five hundred pound? Do I hear five hundred? O.K. Do I hear five?"

Mervyn noticed a few rows from the front a girl with beautiful shining chestnut hair. She stood with her back to him, listening to the proceedings. He edged his way through until he was immediately behind her, the gleaming hair a few inches from his great hook of a nose. He could smell its clean shampoo freshness, and breathed it in so deeply that his head felt light. Abruptly, as though she sensed a disagreeable presence, the girl moved forward three or four places and Mervyn in an instant felt a kind of shame, as though he had been guilty of some indecency.

Wasn't it pathetic - the best he could hope for was to be able to stand close to a pretty girl, to sneak up like some pervert behind a complete stranger. Merv the Perv. That's what they'd called him briefly in his teenage days when he never had a girlfriend, although a glance gave them the real reason. Black thoughts and memories closed round him.

Once, only once, when their adolescent pack was hunting in dancehalls and clubs, had he been sufficiently fortified by beer to ask a girl for a dance: he could still see her expression and hear her cold 'No thank you'. Later he saw her with her friends nodding in his direction, and they giggled and shimmied through the perfumed heat to dance with one another inside their own little select stockade.

Then there had been the fiasco of the Personal Columns experiment. The *fun-loving divorcee with a GSOH* had turned out to be a hard-as-nails freeloader who had stung Mervyn for the most expensive meal and bottle of wine that the restaurant could produce, before promising to 'think it over' and, in all likelihood, moving on to her next victim. Mervyn shuddered at the recollection. From that moment he accepted the inevitable, obliged to watch as his mates 'chatted up' and 'saw home' and made dates. In the encounter of the sexes his job was to hold the coats.

He was on the point of going home before the auction had got into full swing when he remembered why he came to the auction in the first place, and decided to stay at least a little longer. Saturday afternoon was when Aunt Shirley, his mother's relentless twin sister, came round.

"And when are you going to get yourself a nice girlfriend, Mervyn?" as though they were to be had off the shelf at the local convenience store. He could hardly tell her he would have been pleased with any girlfriend, never mind a nice one. "There must be plenty of girls looking for a nice boy like you," was her usual finish, and Mervyn felt it was more a rebuke than an encouragement.

The galling truth was that in one respect she was right. Any girl who would overlook his appearance and get to know him would indeed find him 'a nice boy'. He used to watch the offhand and selfish ways his pals treated their girlfriends, and knew that in their place he would have been so much more caring, so much more considerate. He had never been given the chance. That old claim that it wasn't looks that mattered, but personality, was a cruel lie designed to comfort losers. If only he could get started. Yes, that was it, getting started. It was the same kind of frustration he used to feel as a child playing *Snakes and Ladders*, when others were racing ahead towards the finish and he couldn't throw a 6 to get going. Now all his pals were married, some for the second time, and he wasn't even in the game.

Mervyn had idly picked up a vase, Lot 27, and was looking at it without seeing it when a voice beside him said, "Nice, isn't it?" He half turned, not sure if the remark had been made to him, and saw a vision beside him. It was in the form of a girl about twenty, with fair hair, or blonde, he never knew the difference, wide eyes, and the loveliest mouth he had ever seen.

"I love oriental vases," the vision continued, and smiled, and the words were definitely meant for him.

Never having been spoken to this way by any girl, and now to be addressed by the kind of girl who lived mostly in his romantic fantasies, Mervyn was taken completely off guard. He was almost equally surprised to hear his own voice saying, "Yes, yes, it is nice." Next thing she was chatting freely to him about auctions and vases and prices, as though his nose were perfectly normal and his ears not objects of ridicule. The experience was unprecedented, unaccountable. Mervyn wasn't sure afterwards if he managed any part in the conversation, his mouth dry as it was, and his heart thumping.

"It's been lovely talking to you," the girl finished, preparing to move off. "It's so warm in this crowd. I'm going to see if I can get a drink somewhere."

He almost missed it, he almost let it slip. The kind of moment he had prayed for and dreamed about for half his life, and he almost let it slip. Once again, however, a voice that sounded like his spoke in his head and he heard it say, "I could do with a drink myself." Then he was leading her to the back of the room where a corner stall was providentially placed to enable a breathless man to buy a soft drink for a living goddess.

"And what can I get you and your young lady, sir?" the man asked, and Mervyn would have given him any price for the two Cokes he ordered.

"I'm Nancy, by the way," she smiled between sips, and he noticed a precious, tiny little gap between her front teeth.

"I'm Mervyn," and he remembered just in time not to spoil the moment by offering a sweaty hand. "Are you going to bid for the vase?"

"I don't know. It'll probably make more than a student grant would allow. Are you interested in anything, Mervyn?"

What was happening? Was he ill and delirious? A truly beautiful girl had just spoken his name in the same natural easy tone that he used to envy when he heard it used for others, and thought never to hear for himself.

And the coincidence of the Lot number, 27, the same as his age. Was some kind Fate finally compensating him for all those years of misery...

"No, I'm a window shopper who's come in from the cold," and she laughed at his joke and he felt a kind of thrill not unlike fear. "If that vase is number 27 we'll better get back and stake our claim."

For a moment he felt he had been presumptuous in his use of 'we' and 'our', but the easy way she accepted it touched Mervyn with new feelings he couldn't have described.

They were back in good time, but soon Lot 26, a portable sewing machine, had been knocked down for a tenner, and the vase was being displayed at the front by the sad-looking man in the tan overall.

"Lot 27," announced the auctioneer. "A fine vaze, vaz, or voz, or all three together. Three for the price of one. Who'll start me at a fiver?"

Nancy had her mouth open to oblige when Mervyn called out 'Five' in a professional tone. The auctioneer looked mildly surprised, as if he thought he might have had to go lower to get started. He was about to go through the 'any advance' routine when someone at front left suddenly called 'Ten'. The hint of surprise on the auctioneer's face firmed up, and he glanced at the vase again, wondering if it had a value that had escaped him. Mervyn hesitated, but only for a moment, and came back with 'Twelve'.

He peered through the blur of faces and located his adversary just as he countered with 'Fifteen'. The man was in his forties, of slim build, slightly balding, nondescript. He wore a dark polo neck pullover below a grey tweed jacket. He looked steadily ahead, taking no interest in whoever was bidding against him.

"Twenty." The word was out of Mervyn's mouth before his mind had licensed it, and he felt an anxious courage as battle was joined.

"Thirty."

The buzz of interest that had started now grew louder, and Mervyn experienced the same kind of nervous pride he had felt years ago at primary school when an excited crowd had gathered in an instant to watch him in a schoolyard fight.

"Don't, Mervyn, please don't, it's not worth it," pleaded Nancy at his side, but the gratitude and concern in her lovely upturned face cancelled out completely the import of her words. Mervyn swallowed hard and with only a slight tremor in his voice returned his opponent's strike with a resolute 'Thirty five'.

"Thirty five, I'm hearing thirty five, I've got thirty five for Lot 27, I'm hearing thirty five for the vase. Are there any more bids...is the bidding closed at thirty five?"

"Forty five."

The words hit Mervyn in the stomach like a battering ram, and the murmur in the hall rose to a rumble. Even the little veteran auctioneer held his breath. The only unmoved one in the room was he who had caused the sensation, the balding head steady, not a tremble in the anonymous face, the stance secure. Mervyn by contrast felt his right leg start to shake, just as it used to do before exams or badminton finals, or at interviews. He sensed every eye on him in expectation and felt caught up in a situation that was way out of his depth. How could he lose face now in full public gaze and, most importantly, how would he appear to Nancy?

Yet that man unnerved him: he was so calm, so detached, a professional, and who knew how far he would be prepared to go to get the vase? As doubts and fears swirled round in Mervyn's head something slid into his hand and he realized that he was holding the little fingers of the loveliest girl in the world, and in that moment all uncertainties disappeared: the cost of a vase, or anything else the auction room could offer, was as important as a grain of sand in a desert.

"Fifty." His challenge cut through the babble that was starting up, and he felt Nancy's hand tighten on his in the tension as he swung a look across at his rival. The man hadn't moved a muscle.

"Fifty. Fifty pounds for the vase, there's fifty bid on the vase. Are we all finished at fifty? Have we any more bids for the vase? It's going at fifty once...it's at fifty twice..." The pause lasted for another 27 years..........."Sold, sold at fifty pounds, it's gone at fifty pounds."

Mervyn's head swam, not because of the little burst of ragged applause that broke out, but because at the moment of the sale Nancy, still holding his hand, had stretched up, like a child to her daddy, and kissed him on the cheek.

Somehow he controlled his relief and joy and managed to say in a voice that trembled, in spite of his best efforts,"Well, we got it, we got it after all. Hold on a minute and I'll settle things up," and then he was on his way to the little partitioned office, his mind sprinting ahead to picnics and valentine cards and mufflered walks in the mountains.

If only Darren Mason could have been there at that moment. He had never been able to forget the evening when his 'friend' Darren, handsome Darren, the dream boy of every girl in the senior school, had spilt both his drink and the truth, right in front of him, that he liked Mervyn for a mate because his own good looks were even better when seen against Mervyn's ugliness. The pain of it came back sharp as ever, even when he was paying for the vase, but now it no longer mattered. No, now he was started, he'd thrown his six, or it had been thrown for him, and he was going to climb ladders all the way, and slide down not even one little snake.

Nancy wasn't where he had left her. A terrible cold fear, almost a panic, paralysed his mind. He checked the refreshments stall area and returned, still clutching the vase, to the spot where they had stood.

"You remember the girl with me, the girl with the fair hair?" he asked a woman in a wrinkled red cardigan. "Did you see where she went?"

"She's away," said the woman, more interested in a vacuum cleaner held up for show.

"Away? What d'you mean 'away'? Away where?" Mervyn could feel a burning starting in his neck and spreading over his face.

"How would I know? Away home maybe. She went out, that's all I know."

Mervyn rushed over to the big dirty window that looked down into the street. He saw them just as they reached the car. Nancy, or whatever her name was, was touching up her lipstick. Had he been close enough he would have heard her partner remarking, "These Pound Shop vases are doin' the business, love. We'll maybe try another one on Tuesday, over at Gavenden."

MEDIUM RARE

"You know I love you, Diane. Whatever you think, right or wrong, good or bad, you know I love you." His candlelit face confirmed the earnestness of the words. She dropped her eyes and gently withdrew the hand his fingers had imprisoned on the table.

He waved away a hovering waiter. "Yes, I know it's only six weeks, but, six weeks or six years, we are meant for each other, Diane. I believe in Fate bringing people together. That's why we met. We were destined to meet at the bereavement counselling meetings, I've never been more sure of anything."

She kept her eyes lowered, but her tone was firm. "Please don't rush things, Derek. I feel I shouldn't be here with you like this so soon after the accident. It feels wrong. Bill has been dead only four months. The inquest isn't even over, and here I am with you as if he'd never existed. And your poor wife, her months of suffering. It just seems wrong. I feel guilt or shame or something. I keep wondering how Bill would feel about all this."

"He doesn't blame you at all, he wants you to be happy."

She looked up sharply. "Don't say things like that."

He hesitated, feeling the rebuke, but continued. "I know he approves, I know you are not to feel you are doing something wrong."

Diane turned away. "How can you say that? Every day I'm surrounded by his things, his books, his clothes, his fishing rods, everything. I've made my mind up, I'm going to put the house up for sale. For me it's like a scrapbook of Bill's life. I feel too guilty even to invite you home, Derek, and you're saying I should feel I'm doing nothing wrong. And how can you have forgotten Alison so quickly?" In the soft light the anguish showed in her delicate, well-bred face.

Suddenly he folded the menus flat and trapped both her hands on the table. "Diane, there's something you have to hear, you must please listen." His voice was hoarse. "When I said I know that Bill approves, I meant it literally. I know, yes, know, that both Bill and Alison give their blessing to our relationship."

Diane's mouth opened in surprise, but before she could say anything he was rushing on. "You see, I've been in touch with them, or they've been in touch with me. They've spoken to me, not directly, but through a medium. I've been to a spiritualist, Diane, a medium, a genuine man, a good man. Please believe me, both Alison and Bill are happy and they want us to be happy together.

No, wait, please, it's true. I'm not a fool, Diane, I'm not being conned, it's not just some phoney telling me the things I want to hear. This man is real. He's told me things that nobody knew but Alison and me. It's amazing. You'll see for yourself, you'll believe too. Bill will speak to you, I promise, he'll speak to you, just as Alison spoke to me."

The emotion overtook him and he wiped an eye with his napkin, freeing a hand, but she was too dazed to withdraw it. They sat in silence, Diane unable to reply.

"You must go and see this spiritualist, for your own sake, no matter about me, about us. Go with me, or go by yourself, but please go, for your own peace of mind."

Diane freed her other hand and laced her fingers together, her expression uncomfortable. "I'm sorry, Derek, but I just don't believe in these things. I never have. I've always avoided fortunetellers and palm readers and horoscopes, all that kind of stuff. I can't take any of it seriously. I'm surprised you do."

"I didn't, not until a week ago, but there's Fate again. Can I tell you what happened? It was last Tuesday evening. I was driving home, and there happened to be one of those chat or call-in programmes on the radio, you know the kind of thing.

Well, the subject was the spirit world, contacting the dead, something I'd never seriously thought about in my life before. I was only half listening, thinking about other things, but then a detective came on and he spoke about this spiritualist who had helped them solve two murders, two crimes where they had no clues and no suspects. It was amazing. The detective was totally convinced, and he said that all his police colleagues, hard cynics every one of them, were convinced as well.

At the end of the programme anybody interested or wanting further information was invited to phone in. I couldn't get it out of my mind, Diane, and the next day I called the Radio Station and they were permitted to give out the spiritualist's number. I rang him, and the following evening I went to a meeting. He doesn't like the term séance. It wasn't anything like I'd imagined, it was just a group of ordinary people wanting for different reasons to get in touch with someone who had passed over. There, you see, I'm using their terms already."

Derek gave a short laugh at his own expense but his mood was totally serious.

"I felt right away that this was real, that there was nothing fake about it. There's something humble and caring about the man, and he doesn't make great claims about himself. He admitted from the start that there might be people there he couldn't help, and that he might be contacted by people on the other side who had no connection with anybody in the room.

Suddenly, Diane, and the shock of it nearly stopped my heart, he was talking about me, and Alison's cancer, and how I had to keep watering her flower boxes, and the new wooden flooring we had been talking about just before she went into hospital. He mentioned other things, little things, things nobody but Alison and I knew about. It was incredible. He said it was a woman speaking to him, and I knew it was Alison; there was nobody else it could have been, no other way he could have known those things.

She told me she was happy, and that I was close to happiness, and I wasn't to worry. She said the person who was going to make me happy was not to be anxious, that it was all right. Diane, the tears were rolling down my face, and other people in the room were crying too."

"How much was it?" asked Diane, trying to control a voice that was trembling and noticeably softened.

"That's another thing. There's no actual charge. People give according to their means and to their own feelings of gratitude. I don't mind telling you that I gave him fifty quid and I would have doubled that if I had had it with me. But there's no use me telling you all this, Diane. The only way you'll believe me is if you go yourself..."

"If you're expecting a crystal ball, spooky voices and flickering lights, you're going to be disappointed."

They were in one of the side chambers of the Town Hall, its ornate mouldings, trompe l'oeil ceiling of drifting clouds, panelled walls and gilt framed portraits at odds with the fire extinguishers, EXIT signs, and panic doors of the modern public building. The speaker was a middle-aged man in casual clothes. His only remarkable feature was a full head of steel gray hair. The audience was a cluster of anxious looking people, mostly women, the youngest in her thirties.

Diane was disappointed. "He doesn't look too impressive; I imagined a spiritualist would have looked a bit more...spiritual. Where's the table we're meant to sit round?"

"There isn't one. It's not like that. It's not a carnival sideshow," Derek said defensively.

The speaker was continuing. "You don't need to sit in darkness, or hold hands, or close your eyes. I'm going to reduce the lighting to help you relax and think about the one you would like to hear from. Remember, I am just a medium, a means to receive and transmit messages. All I can do is tell you what I hear, if anything."

The lighting dimmed and the people involuntarily shuffled their plastic chairs into a half circle. Diane noticed a woman shiver, as though a chill had passed through her. For a few moments there was silence. The man didn't have his eyes closed, but seemed to be listening intently. When he spoke it was softly, in the manner of an interpreter keeping pace with a foreign speaker.

"Is there someone present who wants to hear from Sean, someone who is worried, unhappy... unhappy that she was not on speaking terms with Sean, someone who wanted to patch things up with him but feels she left it too late."

As the words were being spoken in that odd mimetic manner the woman immediately in front of Derek stiffened and put her hand up to her mouth. She looked like she had been given an electric shock.

"She has left her red setter, Rory, with a neighbour," the voice continued smoothly. "She wears bright clothes but her heart is sad."

The woman started to sob. "Sean, Sean, I'm sorry, Sean, it was all my fault. I haven't enjoyed a single minute since that day. I should have said I was sorry, I should have, I should have." Her voice trailed off in grief.

"You are not to worry. It is worry that has given you the ulcer. Sean loves you, you are still his little sister, the little sister with the pigtails. He is happy. There is nothing to forgive. Sean knows you love him. He asks if you can remember the name of the little yellow duck he won for you at the fairground."

"Sukie, it was Sukie," the woman sobbed, her love for her brother shining through the blotchiness of her face, her heart open with tenderness. One or two people in the audience were visibly moved by her flood of emotion.

"Is Diane here?" the medium suddenly asked, and Derek sat forward in his chair, the muscles in his jaw tensing. "I need to speak to Diane. Is Diane here with us today?"

"Yes." It was Derek who answered. Diane looked too stunned to speak for herself. The medium was unperturbed. "Diane, Bill is here. Why are you worrying about him? He knows you are anxious, but you are to forget about the accident and remember him with love. He suffered no pain. The blood you saw on the road was just rusty water from the lorry's radiator. He wants you to know he is happy. He wants you now to take the happiness that is being offered by someone who loves you."

Diane suddenly got up, overturning her chair, and rushed out through the side door. Derek found her in the lobby, trembling. He put his arms round her and she let her head sink on his shoulder. He gently stroked her hair.

"I'm sorry, Derek, I'm sorry, I just couldn't listen any more. It's so frightening, so strange. I'm so confused."

"Ssshh, ssshh, of course you're confused. That's just how I felt when Alison spoke to me. It's hard taking in what's happened…Sssshh, I know, I know."

"Yessir, here's to me," and the medium raised his glass to himself. Without the grey wig he looked even more nondescript. "We're home and dry on this one."
'Derek' didn't join in the toast, but he was equally satisfied. "Friday evening's the clincher. It's her birthday and I'm going to celebrate it in style. Wining, dining, and then the sparkler. She's a class lady, Leonard, so it'll be the real thing, a five grand diamond, none of your Zircon stuff for my Diane."
"Listen to you," said Leonard. "There's my little team away back in the train, happy with their sandwiches and the fifty quid in their pocket, and you're splashing out five big ones on a rock. I could get you one for a coupla hundred."
'Derek' smiled. "Don't spoil the ship for a ha'p'orth of tar, Lennie old son. Remember that, when I've got my hands on dear old Bill's two hundred grand life insurance."
"The sooner the better," grumbled Lennie. "I'm sick of this town. It's about time we moved on. Anyhow, if you want to be the big spender, I'll have another pint."

Derek was on a high. The champagne, the meal, the surprise birthday cake, and then the presentation of the ring with the proposal. His face glowed as he refilled their glasses. "To us, darling, to our lives together. I'll never order another medium rare without thinking how much I owe to a rare medium." He was pleased with the inversion. Suddenly his voice was husky. "Seeing you wearing that ring makes me the happiest man in the world, and I can say that now without any other feelings to spoil it."
Diane smiled and didn't reply, but stretched wide her left hand in that universal signal of a woman newly engaged.
"You'll have to excuse me, darling, but I can't hold my champagne." He laughed, and headed for the Gents to phone Leonard and confirm the triumph. It was the last time he ever saw his fiancée.

"For the first time in my whole career I nearly laughed out loud and gave the game away. I had to run out to get my face straight." 'Diane' giggled. She was in bed with Anita, her lover. "You should have seen the antics of that medium, in touch with the dead husband I had invented. And that ridiculous creature sobbing 'Sean, Sean'. The whole thing was hilarious. Pure 'Amateur Night' stuff. Wonder if I'll get as much fun the next time I decide to be bereaved?"

"It's a lovely ring." Anita cuddled up close. She laughed. "The things men will do for money."

WITHERED

Edith wondered briefly if there was a word opposite to shrine, a word for a place of brooding and restlessness of soul. She sat down in front of the photograph on her dressing table and once more asked herself *Why me?* The question had become a plaint, to be spoken aloud in the silence of her lonely bedroom: *Why me*, and sometimes *Why not me*, as she faced the smiling photograph of herself arm in arm with Natalie, her identical twin sister. Yes, identical, completely indistinguishable from each other. Even their voices were entirely alike, as a trial test for a new voice-operated security system had scientifically proved. Ironic, then, that the Templeton twins, so totally matched in sight and sound, were worlds apart in everything else.

The picture showed two young women in their late twenties, attractive without being pretty, with the same wavy auburn hair and the same slightly retroussé noses that somebody had once described as 'cutesy'. The photo had been taken 18 months earlier, just days before their mother had died so suddenly at the supermarket from a massive coronary.

Edith raised her eyes from the image and looked at herself in the oval dressing table mirror. How could she look just the same when everything else in her life had changed so terribly, and how could so much have happened in just over a year?

First Sam Bradfield had arrived, it seemed from nowhere, and was going out with Natalie, seriously going out with Natalie. In a matter of weeks they were engaged, a few months later they were married, and only a few after that they were living in South Africa. Sam was that kind of man, purposeful, knowing what he wanted and wasting no time in going for it.

Edith was just starting to adapt to living at home with only her father when he suffered a stroke. It left him partly paralysed down one side, a little doddery, and with his speech slurred.

Why was everything falling to pieces? Overnight Edith had to give up the job she enjoyed at the local Tax Office to become a full time carer.

When photos of a lovely house and swimming pool in Cape Town started arriving, together with details of wealth, sunny weather, and leisurely lifestyle, Edith's slide into the dark deeps of self pity and bitterness was rapid and unchecked. She was honest enough to recognise that these feelings were not entirely new, but they were now hardened by an accompanying sense of injustice and resentment.

For as long as she could remember, she had envied her twin sister. There was none of the traditional sibling rivalry that some families grew up with, because there was absolutely no competitive spirit in Natalie, but from her early childhood Edith felt that her sister was the favourite, no matter how much her parents tried to disguise their preference.

Even their names, in Edith's view, were not fairly balanced. Her own was dry, dull, its letters reminding her somehow of *withered*, while *Natalie* was a name like dark rich chocolate. There was no denying the differences in the two girls' personalities: they were the proverbial chalk and cheese. Edith was withdrawn, diffident, Natalie outgoing, happy-go-lucky, always having a good time, more popular at school and with their friends.

A scene stuck in Edith's mind, clear as yesterday. She saw herself, a young woman of eighteen, sitting like a child on her bed sobbing, "It's not fair, it's not fair." They had just got their exam results from college. She had studied hard, and revised long dreary hours, perhaps motivated by an eagerness to do better than her sister. Natalie, by contrast, 'crammed' the night before each exam, gambling on one or two questions coming up. They did. Although Edith's results were excellent and she could have regarded herself as being better informed and educated, she couldn't be consoled when she learned that overall she was in second place to Natalie.

For the first time she tasted in full the cruelty of an unfair world...........

She couldn't think of one good reason to turn the invitation down. When Natalie's long letter arrived asking her sister over to Cape Town for a break, a holiday, Edith's first instinct was to refuse; Natalie just wanted to show off her good fortune, to rub her nose in it, to put the boot in, to salve her own conscience. In her heart Edith knew none of this was true, that it was the working of her own embittered mind, that her sister would never have considered these things for a moment. The sentiments were genuine:

You need a holiday, Edith. If you can make the arrangements your side to get dad into a good nursing home for a couple of weeks, we'll take care of all the expenses. Now, don't be insulted or start all that silly pride stuff, but we want to pay for your flight. You've earned it, Edith; you must be exhausted, poor soul. Anyhow, I'm a bit homesick now and again, and I'd love to see you for my own sake as well as yours. Don't even think of saying you can't, we won't take No for an answer.

The 'exhausted' part was bang on target. Edith's father wore her out physically, and she felt close to nervous exhaustion as well, especially facing the growing fear that he was becoming incontinent. The prospect of being free of that weight of responsibility, if only for a short period, was enough to overrule any counter arguments that even her blackest mood might produce...

They were finally alone together. Sam and Natalie had picked Edith up the previous evening from the airport, but she was so tired from the travelling and the heat that she had gone to bed immediately without even seeing round the house. Next morning she woke in a strange room to the soft whirring of a ceiling fan. A thick towelling dressing gown was waiting for her in the en suite bathroom. Edith felt like she was in a 5 star hotel....

"It's good seeing you, Edith, really good. I want to hear everything, about dad, about yourself, the town, any local news, any gossip."

Breakfast and the tour of the house were over, and the sisters were sitting out on the patio, palm trees throwing spear patterns over the warm tiles. Sam had left for work at eight, 'eight on the dot'. Natalie opened a bottle of best South African red.

There was something different about her, something Edith at first could not identify. Apart from the little boomerang scar a firework had imprinted on Edith's wrist, there were no distinguishing marks to identify either girl. Edith had expected her sister to be deeply tanned, but there was no noticeable change in her complexion. She studied Natalie as she rambled on about the different climate and ways of doing things that she had had to get used to. Suddenly she knew what was changed. There was no sparkle. Their mother used to joke that the only way she could tell the difference between them was the sparkle in Natalie's eyes, a real sparkle, an actual sparkle, eloquent of spirit and personality. That sparkle was missing, as distinctly as a severed finger.

"If it's social chit-chat you're looking for," said Edith when Natalie returned to the theme of things back home, "you're asking the wrong person. All I know about are medicines and bills and housework."

Although she was speaking to her own sister, Edith felt at a social disadvantage. Prosperity was in evidence all around, from the cook who had served breakfast and the gardener now cutting the hedge, down to the finest crystal wineglasses. Natalie topped up Edith's glass, but not her own.

As the women talked and the heat built up Edith made a staggering, a sensational discovery - Natalie, the vivacious, laughing, popular Natalie, the Natalie the gods had always smiled on, was unhappy. It was heretical, it was contrary to all known experience, but how could she doubt it when she was hearing it straight from source.

"Remember we used to turn straight to the Problem Page in the women's magazines? Well, I'm the 'lonely wife', Edith. Sam's business comes first, he's your classic workaholic. I'm expected to sit here every day and be happy because he's making lots of money. I go nowhere, do nothing, I've no friends, no social life, I'm not allowed to take a job, I'm rusting away. Look, I can't even have a second glass of wine. I'm on anti-depressants." She leaned closer. "There's something else, Edith. Sam wants children, a son, but we've found out I can't have any. Nothing can be done. I think deep inside he blames me. So how do you like them apples?"

Edith felt a slow thrill of satisfaction as she realised the extent of her sister's discontent. What was she wanting, sympathy? Sitting there in luxury and leisure, with a husband and house and servants, and looking for sympathy. Was that why she had been flown over, to listen to the bleating of her spoiled sister? Let her spend a day or two in her shoes, tending to her father and doing the cooking and washing and ironing and shopping, without a word of thanks. Let her try a bit of that, and then she would see who was well off.

"I'm sorry things aren't working out, Natalie," she said coldly, "but there are a lot of people worse off than you are."

As the two weeks went by Edith saw ample evidence of the empty marriage of her sister. She saw no tenderness between husband and wife, and equally no acrimony, no fire. That was it, there was nothing between Sam and Natalie, just a desert of emotional indifference. For her part, Edith felt the distance between Natalie and herself, if anything, increase. She saw little to blame in Sam Bradfield. He was a hard worker and solid provider, a steady character, a generous man who deserved gratitude and received none. Sam and she got on very well, very well indeed.

Dr. Stewart decided to try her with Tamazopan. He had been the family doctor for over thirty years, and could remember the proud mother pushing the little twin girls in a double tansad through the town.

He could understand Edith's emotional state: the sudden loss of the mother, the loneliness when her sister had married and emigrated, the father's stroke. It was easy being wise after the event, of course, but Edith's depression seemed to have started soon after she came back from that trip to South Africa. Fortunately she was still physically sound, but the sleeplessness, anxiety and loss of appetite could soon change that. Respite care was difficult, but he'd see about getting her some help in the house, or arrange for a nurse or social worker to call regularly to assist with the old man. In the meantime the medication should steady the ship....

It was a shock for the doctor six weeks later when he was told about the attempted suicide. Fortunately Edith had made the attempt on her own life on Tuesday, the day the visiting nurse called. She had been found unconscious in her bedroom, overdosed on paracetamol, with her father watching racing on TV downstairs, unaware of the near tragedy above him. By good fortune the front door was open when Nurse Cardwell arrived. The suicide attempt was an amateur job, but Dr Stewart was seriously alarmed by the intention. He resolved to get in touch with her sister in South Africa to apprise her of his concern, and determined that when Edith was released from hospital he would have to review the whole caring situation for the old man. How would Edith do on Prozac?

Well, it seemed. A careful official eye was kept on both father and daughter, nonetheless, in the weeks that followed. Edith was given regular appointments so that Stewart could assess her progress. The house was now visited every day by a home help, and, as often as resources would allow, by a stroke specialist nurse and social worker.

As for Edith's married sister in South Africa, Stewart called with Mr Templeton and got permission from the old man to contact her. Natalie was distressed when she was told what had happened, and wanted to come home at once, but finally agreed to wait until the doctor judged Edith ready to cope. Edith was informed, and raised no objections. A month after the incident the doctor was of the view that Edith was sufficiently recovered from her depression to receive her visitors, and they duly arrived that same weekend.

What followed stayed with Dr Stewart the remainder of his professional life, and beyond. He got the phone call from the police shortly after nine o'clock on the Wednesday morning.

The undertaker, two paramedics, two police officers and a WPC were there already, the latter trying to comfort the totally distraught sister. A man he assumed was her husband stood awkwardly behind her chair, at a loss. Her old father was trying to drink a cup of tea from a hand that shook uncontrollably.

A glance was enough, but Stewart conducted the medical examination just the same. Edith had made no mistake this time. Her fully clothed body lay the length of the bed, a twisted yawn having formed in death, little red burst-bubble rings at each side of the mouth. A glass, an empty bottle of tablets, an open bottle of wine, and a corkscrew bottle opener were on the bedside table. These items were neatly set in a row. Stewart had been present at a number of such scenes down the years, but on this occasion he felt like some kind of desecrator as the others watched him at work.

When he had finished and come downstairs, he was met by Natalie's husband, who reached out a hand.

"I'm Sam Bradfield. Thanks for coming so quickly, doctor. This is a terrible tragedy. I'm a bit worried about my wife, she's in a bad state. She's trembling non-stop. Would you have a look at her?"

Natalie was crouched in the chair sobbing, shaking, her face blotched and ugly in grief. She kept repeating, "It's my fault, it's all my fault," as the doctor was giving her a sedative.

The autopsy established that the death of Edith Templeton had been caused by respiratory failure produced by an overdose of anti-histamine tablets, their effect accelerated by interaction with anti-depressant drugs already present in the system. Her funeral and cremation two days after the post mortem was a sad, private little affair. Natalie wept throughout the brief ceremony. Her father seemed only partly aware of what was happening.

"I'll call you later, Mrs Bradfield," said the worn little resident chaplain, sympathetic and thinking of his fee, but Natalie seemed not to hear him and walked away, red-eyed and fragile, supported by her husband.

Sam Bradfield and his wife stayed a further week, long enough to tidy up Edith's affairs, see Mr. Templeton accepted into an expensive Private Nursing Home, and the family home and contents in the hands of a solicitor. At that point Sam simply had to be back in Cape Town for his business. Natalie wanted to follow him out later, but he insisted she go with him. They were to return for the inquest as soon as the coroner had set a date.

Dr Stewart was a primary witness three months later. Edith's sister sat with her husband just a few feet from him in the small Coroner's Court. She looked tense and tired, and kept her head down. Somehow he was glad not to meet her eye.

The post mortem report revealed that death would have occurred in less than 5 minutes. The police sergeant in attendance at the scene told the inquest jury how the shells of 20 Piraton capsules had been found in a wastepaper basket beside the bed, and that forensic examination of the wineglass also found at the scene showed that the contents of the capsules had been mixed into a glass of red wine, apparently taken from a bottle on the bedside table. The coroner asked a few questions about the availability of the drug, the incidence of its use in such deaths, and the degree of pharmaceutical knowledge that would be needed to use the drug to such an end.

The home help lady had seen no marked alteration in the deceased's mood or behaviour the previous day, but described her general manner as 'sometimes a bit jittery and sometimes a bit dull'. This description was corroborated by the social worker, who hadn't seen Miss Templeton that particular day, but was familiar with her from a series of regular visits.

A deposition by Mr Templeton was read to the jury, as the superintendent of the Nursing Home did not judge him fit to be present at the Inquest. It added little to the proceedings beyond stating that Edith had been a good daughter and very kind to him, and he was sorry if he had been a nuisance to her. Stewart noticed Mrs Bradfield wiping her eyes as her father's statement was read aloud.

In her own evidence Natalie stated how she and her husband had spent three days with her sister and her father. She had found her sister changed since they had last seen each other, in South Africa. She seemed lethargic and debilitated, but Natalie had put this down to the effects of the medication she was taking. She described the events of the Tuesday evening in a voice that trembled on the edge of weeping.

"We were talking about dad, and how he seemed to be making no improvement, and had lost all heart in living, and then I said it, I said the wrong thing, but, honestly, I didn't intend any criticism, I was thinking only of what was best for poor Edith."

Natalie broke into a sob as she appealed to the court for understanding. "I didn't mean any harm, I just said that we should put dad into a Home where he could be properly looked after. Yes, I said 'properly looked after', but I wasn't blaming Edith or anybody, I just wanted dad and Edith to get what was best for both of them, and I should have been more careful what I said, and look what's happened…I'll never forgive myself. After all she'd done, and her not being well, and me away in another country, and what had already happened, and I'm saying 'properly looked after'….

You should have seen her poor little face………..she couldn't take it, she couldn't take any more, and I'm to blame, but I swear I didn't mean it, I'd give anything not to have said it……….." She was shuddering in guilt and sorrow.

When Dr Stewart came to give his report, however, it seemed that any intimation of blame had been reserved for him.

"And in your professional judgement, Dr Stewart, a person being treated for depression, a person with a history of attempted suicide, was suitable to take care of a partly disabled parent…

And Piraton are available over the counter? And the maximum dose is 6 capsules daily? And did you know if your patient was on any medication other than you had prescribed?

So there are a number of anti-depressants available? It's very much a matter of hit and miss, then, trying them out to see which works best for each individual patient?

And you were confident that the Prozac were working, that there was little likelihood of another suicide attempt?

And you believed that your patient was in a fit state, physically and emotionally, to look after two visitors, as well as her incontinent and confused father.........."

The Verdict was *Suicide while the balance of the mind was disturbed*. Dr Stewart was relieved that the Bradfields afterwards showed no inclination at all to blame him in any way. They were catching a flight next morning, and planned to spend all the time they could with old Mr Templeton.

They parted on the steps of the Court House, a chill wind whipping up and a few drops of rain slicing down. As Mrs Bradfield shook hands with the doctor and thanked him for all he had done, the cuff of her coat slid over a faint little boomerang scar on her wrist.

SOLD

"There's a fabulous view from the big window here, right into the next county... This side of the house faces due west, so you get a lovely sunset... The house has been completely redecorated, inside and out."

The agent was in full flow. Rose despised her thin enthusiasm, her 'corporate image' uniform, her clipboard. She wished this so-called professional could be there in a day or two to see the job done properly.

Rose's contempt had been fired initially by how easily the woman had fallen for Eddie's upper class act: Eddie, with the carefully combed hair parting and Clark Gable moustache, the cravat and sports jacket, the cavalry twill trousers and suede shoes. He was like a caricature of the leading men he had so often played in those phoney Noel Coward plays, which the public unaccountably never seemed to tire of. If this jabbering little woman, so easily impressed, could only be in their cheap hotel room for a few minutes to see him in his string vest putting on his Grecian 2000...

She called across the empty room to him, "Clive, darling, did you remember to bring the measuring thing? I want to check if our lounge curtains at Rexford would be suitable here." Rose knew that disregard for money, at any level of society, aroused suspicion, whereas careful economy earned respect and credibility.

"What measuring thing? Oh, don't start all that business now, Pamela. You know I've an appointment at three."

The little tiff that followed was easy stuff for two professionals. The woman in the beige company suit discreetly looked out of the big window until she judged the moment right.

"Excuse me, I've got a measuring tape in the car. Could I slip out for it? That is, if it's all right with you."

Eddie allowed himself to be ruled by the third party. "Thank you, that will do well. This lady is organised, Pamela, organised. I'm sure there's a lesson there for anyone who might care to take it."

The 'lady', pleased but hiding it from Rose, set down her clipboard, brochure and key and went out in professional triumph.

"Hurry up, Eddie. She's a keen one."

Eddie snatched up the key, produced a flat tin tobacco box filled with wax, and made an imprint of both sides of the key. The job was done in seconds...

The gullibility of the public: where would they be without it? Rose used to find herself wondering how their victims could be so easily taken in by Eddie's transparent persona, or, for that matter, by her own. The explanation, she had finally decided, was the one Eddie's Professor Higgins had offered to her Eliza Doolittle, before the repertory company had bitten the dust – pronunciation. As soon as the ordinary people heard that detached, faintly languid, accent of the aristocracy, which Eddie and she could produce at the drop of a hat, defences dropped and doors opened, in this case quite literally.

He slipped the big BMW into top gear. The car was the most beautiful, most reliable, most lovable thing in his life. It had been the biggest single investment Rose and he had made when the theatre had closed its doors and they had decided to set up as full-time con artists. Rose had fought against such a financial leap of faith, but Eddie had beaten down all her opposition, arguing that the BMW was their 'collateral'. He had been right, of course, and although she put in the occasional whine about the monthly payments, she liked the style and identity the car gave them.

Eddie loved cleaning it, inside and out, and regularly changing the number plates when new jobs came along. It was his only form of exercise. In return, the BMW was the closest thing he had to a friend; 42 years old, and he couldn't claim to have a real friend in the world. Whenever he wanted to be on his own Eddie would slip away and settle in the car's generous upholstery.

It was probably a throwback to his childhood; as a boy he used to love sitting in the driving seat of his father's big old Vauxhall Wyvern, pretending to be Fangio or Stirling Moss, lovely leathery and ciggy smells all around him. Now, the actor in him would recite to the silently listening dashboard his everyday plans and points of view. Better that, than trying to explain things to Rose. They could see eye to eye on virtually nothing.

The previous day's little disagreement was a case in point: "These public servants really get up my nose. Getting paid to do a job and never doing it. How many of them return your call, for example? As soon as you hear 'leave that with me' or 'I'll get back to you this afternoon', you know what it means - you have to ring them. And what happens then? They're 'out of the office' or 'not in work today' or 'on another call' or 'on leave' or 'at a meeting'. Half the world seems to be 'at a meeting'. It doesn't matter, of course, because 'if you leave a message they'll get back to you'. It makes me mad. They're liars, every last one of them." Eddie had worked himself into the makings of a lather.

Rose had snorted. "I don't believe what I'm hearing. You, you of all people, calling people liars. You're lying every day for a living and you expect honesty from everybody else. That's a laugh."

"Yes, but that's my whole point. I'm doing my job and doing it well. Lying is what we do; we're doing our job, what we're supposed to do. Nobody could say we're neglecting our work. These people aren't doing their job. They're worse liars than we are."

It had been no use. "Rose doesn't have the intellect to see these things," he had confided to the dashboard.

So there he was, self-employed, but without the freedom to choose his colleagues. No, given a choice he would never have chosen Rose to work with, but where else could he find someone as good at her job? A man may choose his company, it would seem, but not his workmates. The dashboard listened in silence.

Eddie returned to the business in hand. "I'll get the key cut first thing in the morning. All we need now is the right client. You'll have to..."

"You leave that to me," she broke in, touching up her nail varnish. "Nobody needs to tell me my job."

She picked an Estate Agent's at random, well away from the first one. Apart from the blue staff uniforms, it was hardly distinguishable from the previous one. The place smelt of stationery and new carpet. Rose was looking her best: the expensive trouser suit she had bought that morning would be returned in a day or two for a full refund. Her hair and complexion were perfect, a product of her extra duties at the Gaiety in charge of make-up.

She cruised the office. Extravagant claims and descriptions were all around her: *A unique new development of luxurious town houses.* Fine, except that another one exactly the same was probably going up on the other side of town. And how were cold plaster and bare timbers luxurious?

An ideal starter home for an energetic young couple. In simple terms, a semi ruin. These people were no better than Eddie and herself, con artists, liars in smart suits.

She spotted her man as by instinct. He was peering at the monthly property newspaper, trying to match it against the battery of illuminated colour photos round the walls. Rose studied him as she pretended to read the specifications in front of her. He was a small mild-looking man in his fifties, smartly dressed, but not entirely at ease in the fine quality clothes. His manner, sharp and confused at the same time, reminded her of the little pawnbroker she used to go to with her father when she was a child.

She drifted across and stood beside him for a few moments.

"Excuse me, I don't wish to meddle, but I see you're looking at houses in the country."

He turned, surprised. "Yes, yes, I am."

"Well, I'm sure you'll not mind, but sometimes these things happen. Fate and all that. You see, we have our house in the country up for sale at present. I'm actually waiting to see the manager chap here about having a go at moving it for us. The other fellow we have is a bit of a slowcoach. Anyhow, I wondered if by chance it might be the kind of thing you're looking for."

The man seemed nonplussed. "I see."

"I'm not a great one for these agent fellows at the best of times, but Clive wants everything done by the book. I've always believed in business being done directly, if it has to be done at all. All this fuss and nonsense is a real bore. What is it they say, we should try to cut out the middle people. I'm all in favour of that. Saves time, apart from everything else."

Rose spoke with that confident familiarity that paradoxically is often used to strangers in the most exclusive circles. The man was sufficiently encouraged to reply, "Well, I don't see anything here of interest. I suppose it could do no harm to have a look at your house. Where is it? I'd need some details; I mean, is there a leaflet — size and number of rooms and so on."

Rose was pleased he hadn't mentioned price, the mark of someone anxious not to appear vulgar.

"The other agent fellow has leaflets all over the shop, not that they've done much good."

"Well, as you say, sometimes these things work out. Who knows? I'm James Kitchen, by the way. A Kitchen looking for a house."

Rose smiled distantly at his little joke. "How d'you do. I'm Pamela Doulton," and she shook hands.

"Look, there's a nice little place next door and I'm just about ready for my morning dose of caf. Would you care to join me........."

Kitchen was ideal, a self-made man, proud of his achievements, innocently vain about his successes. She heard all about his modest beginnings in the car trade, his ambition as a young man, the expansion, the good business sense that told him when to quit.

He seemed in no hurry to rush matters, clearly enjoying conversation in the Coffee

Shop with this stylish, well-bred lady. His main subject was himself.

For her part, Rose dropped in brief references to the City, the children, public schools, places abroad. She steered the talk gently back on target. "So, much as we love it, we simply had to sell the house and move into town. Since Clive was made Chairman of that wretched Board, he'd been practically living there anyhow. Quite frankly, I was worried he would fall asleep at the wheel coming home late from one of those endless, tiresome meetings."

"Isn't it funny," said Kitchen, "that we're going in different directions, as you might say; you've moved into town, I'm wanting out of it. Going back to my roots, I suppose. I want away from the traffic and noise and the crime. Locks and burglar alarms everywhere is no way to live. When we were children growing up in our little cottage the keys were left in the door all night and nobody thought a thing about it."

"Yes, it's a bit of a nuisance. Clive's golf captain had his home burgled last month and he lost some irreplaceable paintings and jewellery. What a bother." Before Kitchen could sympathise Rose's mobile phone rang. "Sorry, these things can be a damn nuisance, but we can't live without them, it seems. Hello."

It was Eddie, grumpy and impatient. "Well, have you got one yet?"

Rose's face brightened. "Marianne. How lovely." Pause. "Yes, I have."

"Make sure he's a good 'un. We're low on readies."

"Marvellous. Actually, Clive and I are going down this weekend to see Emma and her new pony. She's in one of these gymkhana things again. Could we do coffee on Thursday afternoon? I want to keep the morning free."

"Thursday morning? That's O.K. Is he carrying?"

"Should think so. Yes, splendid, splendid. We're hoping to get over to Italy for a few weeks once we've got this house business tidied up. Sorry, Marianne, but I'm actually with someone at the moment…No, thank heavens, I'm having coffee here in town with a friend."

"Make sure he pays for it," growled Eddie, ending the call.

"Of course, Marianne. Lovely to hear from you. Regards to Simon. Bye."

Kitchen put down the cup he had been discreetly addressing during the phone call. "Sorry, but I couldn't help overhearing you were free on Thursday morning. I wondered, would you maybe have time to give me a quick look round the house?"

Rose examined the blank page of her diary. "How would eleven do? We could be there for eleven."

The directions she gave Kitchen were in the nature of a favour granted. She beckoned the waitress for the bill.

"Please allow me," interposed Kitchen, and she smiled her assent.

Eddie was pleased with her account of the catch, especially that Kitchen himself had asked for the appointment. He even sent Rose up to the bar for another vodka and tonic.

Eddie left the keys in the BMW where Kitchen could see them as he passed. He also left the newly cut key in the front door. He had spent time soiling it to give it a well-used look, and had added it to a bunch of others. In such a good area, residents didn't have to worry about security.........

"If he's here at eleven on the nose it'll be a good sign. Not early to upstage us, not late to keep us waiting. I'll maybe try him with a pick-up." Eddie would let something drop and if Kitchen picked it up they would know he was 'amenable'.

He arrived one minute before the hour. They heard his car through the open front door. Eddie gave a little laugh. "He's paced himself. Now, will he come on in, or knock and wait?"

Rose went to answer the knock on the open door. "Ah, good morning, James. Nice to see you. Do come on through. This is my husband, Clive. Clive, James Kitchen."

Eddie was standing in front of the large marble fireplace and had his pipe going. "How d'you do? You found us easily enough? Splendid. It can be tricky enough on your maiden voyage." His resonant tones and rich tobacco blended in an echo of good breeding around the large empty room. He had already decided there was no need to drop his box of matches.

After a few pleasantries he took the lead. "Look, I'm a poor hand at this kind of thing, I'm afraid. Pamela, James and you are on a better footing, why don't you show him round the Dear Old Place. Or perhaps you'd rather make your own recce?"

James opted for the guided tour, allowing Rose the opening for a performance she herself felt would have earned her star billing. How perfectly she judged the faintest tremor of emotion that slipped through as she pointed out what had been Emma's room, and where Richard had displayed his school cricketing trophies; then the wry memory of all those times Clive had nodded off in his study; best of all, perhaps, the barely perceptible softening of tone in the 'grand room' that had hosted so many wonderful evenings of entertainment with so many dear friends.

Kitchen seemed content to allow her to reminisce, asking none of the questions a potential homebuyer might have been expected to ask. He displayed a more businesslike interest, however, when Eddie rejoined them in the big dining room at the back of the house. He went through some of the details in the leaflet with Eddie, and expressed one or two reservations.

"You needn't worry about the garden, James," Rose assured him. "Our gardener lives just half a mile away, and an excellent fellow he is. We promised we'd recommend him to the new owners."

James was finally satisfied enough to make one or two right noises, especially when Eddie dropped the price in the brochure a couple of thousand.

"To tell you the truth, the house is a bit bigger than what I'd been thinking of, but everything else might suit well. Appreciate you offering to drop down a notch or two."

"One has to be flexible in these things in the interests of all parties. I'd like to hear the agent fellow if he heard my way of doing business," Eddie added with a laugh.

"I like the location," continued Kitchen, "in the country, but less than an hour from town."

Eddie laughed again. "Don't depend on that one, not if you're trying to manoeuvre a BMW through rush hour traffic."

Kitchen had all at once become earnest, purposeful, like a man who has made a decision and is eager to get into action. "Look, I'm not a man to waste time. I'm going to organise a surveyor's report, as a matter of course, but I can tell you right now that I'm definitely interested."

"Good fellow," said Eddie. "We'll leave all the small print to your people. From our side, we'd like to move things along, get up a head of steam, rather than leave it to the fellows in the suits. You know how damnably slow they can be. I think, perhaps, between us we should arrange some little guarantee of intention and let the legal eagles take it from there. If we could settle on some little pledge and turn the tiresome stuff over to them."

"Good idea. I'd like to get something settled here and now and avoid all the rigmarole. Stake my claim, so to speak."

"Excellent. My kind of fellow. Just a token of good faith to get the log jam broken."

Kitchen looked pleased to be party to such a gentleman's agreement. "Hold on and I'll get my cheque book from the car," and he scurried out as though worried they might change their mind.

"Easy peasy," said Rose, when he was gone. "I can pick them."

"By Jove, Pamela, you're right," mocked Eddie. "A fellow might be tempted to take him for ten Grand, but not this chap here. Never spook a client by being too greedy. We'll settle for five."

Kitchen was in no hurry coming back. "What's keeping him, where is he?" asked Eddie, more to himself than to Rose.

"Don't be so common, Eddie. He's filling part of the cheque out first. Etiquette, Eddie, etiquette."

Another minute passed, and no sign of man or chequebook.

"I'm getting a bad feeling here," said Eddie, his voice rising as he spoke. "I'm going to see where he is."

Rose was waiting behind in the empty silence of the bare room when a sound such as she'd never heard in all her years of melodrama came screaming down the hall and shrieked round the walls. For an instant she was paralysed by its terrible intensity. She rushed outside, straight into Eddie, his face white beneath the artificial tan, his mouth trembling.

"My car's away, Rose, my car's away. He's away in my BMW. The bastard's away in my BMW." He was close to sobbing.

A glance told it all – the driveway empty except for a red Renault 5, and the house door, for good measure, missing its bunch of keys. Rose ran over to the car. The label stuck on the dash read *ON HIRE FROM EASTSIDE CAR RENTAL*, and the ignition key was gone. They were stranded.

The big BMW lapped up the miles. Its new owner, recently James Kitchen, relaxed in the generous upholstery and remarked to the silently listening dashboard, "Amateurs. You can spot them a mile off…"

REPAIRS

Things seemed to open up for Joe McCollum the day the bus ran over his foot. Perhaps he had been standing too close to the corner of the pavement, and maybe he shouldn't have been thinking to himself with his eyes closed, as was his habit, but in any case he suddenly felt something rubbing roughly across his chest, and, at the same time as he saw the red blur of the bus inches from his face, he felt a crushing weight on his right foot.

The odd thing was that for a moment Joe felt no pain. He waited for the bus to complete its manoeuvre but then, when he tried to move, a terrible sensation in his foot and leg hit him like a flamethrower. Joe was a man who liked no fuss, and he would certainly have avoided what happened next had it been in his power, but his body knew better and crumpled him to the ground.

How did all those people appear instantly from nowhere, with concerned faces and anxious words like 'heart attack' and 'stroke' and 'ambulance', and where on earth did they get a blanket from so quickly? Nobody thought to ask Joe what was wrong with him, even though he was conscious throughout, and in truth he might have been too embarrassed to deflate the drama by saying, "A bus went over my foot."

A customer had once brought in a shoe and asked Joe to cut the front out of it. The man had broken his big toe and had complained over Joe's little counter, "It's the sorest thing you could have, but you never get any sympathy. As soon as you say you've broken your big toe, people start to laugh." Joe lay quietly as the blanket was spread over him.

Thankfully the paramedic in the ambulance didn't laugh, and understood Joe's suffering and the slight shaking that had sneakily started. "Don't worry, Mr McCollum. It's only mild shock that's doing that. It'll be away in no time. So you're sixty-three: you're a bit old to be having arguments with buses. The first thing we'll do is get this foot of yours x-rayed and see what's what. You just lie there and be glad you don't have to walk to the hospital."

Being wheeled down long corridors and cared for by others was so foreign to everything Joe had always known that he was surprised to find himself almost enjoying the attention. The painkilling injection had done its work, and he lay on the trolley taking note of a world that was as white as his little shoe repair shop was brown and black.

Joe had been shielded for so many years behind the counter and in the tiny workshop at the back that he never thought of himself as related to the bright fast-moving world outside, with all its noise and colour. Most of his customers were men who seemed as drab as the footwear they brought in for repair. Occasionally, very occasionally, young women would come in and Joe would be struck by the contrast between the slender little pieces of footwear they put into his hand and the dull slabs he normally mended. The women would leave behind faint perfumes that quickly gave way to the resident smells of rubber, leather and shoe wax that Joe had breathed for almost fifty years.

The x-ray showed a broken arch, three fractured toes, including the big one, and severe bruising of the front of the foot. The doctor told him there was little that could be done for the toes other than time and rest, but a plaster was required to deal with the broken arch, and Joe would be in hospital for at least five or six weeks.

The lady who admitted Joe seemed really surprised that he had no relations or close friends to bring him pyjamas and various basic items. "And are you sure, Mr McCollum, there's nobody at all I could fill in here, no distant relations or neighbours or the like?"

Joe had sometimes thought about this himself, wondering, for example, what would happen if he were suddenly taken ill?

Every year he neither sent nor received Christmas or birthday cards, but it was not something that concerned him greatly. As he lay that afternoon in hospital pyjamas, his plastered foot strung up high above the bottom of the bed, Joe had more time to reflect on his aloneness in the world. It was highlighted at visiting time when his was the only bed without friends and family clustered round it.

The other patients in the ward, whom he got to know very quickly, were happy to share their visitors with Joe. Their assorted friends and relations would come over to marvel at the kaleidoscope of colours in his bruised toes, and offer him the same fruit, sweets and drinks that cluttered all the little bedside cabinet tops. The men in the other beds dubbed him *Technicolor Toes*, and when they learned he was a shoemaker they made jokes about bus-proof toecaps and pedestrian road-tests and so on. A few asked him if he had got the number of the bus for claim purposes, and Joe had to be careful not to laugh at the daft question, as he knew they meant well.

They also ribbed him about Meta, a cleaner and widow with tight bleached curls and a slight stammer. Joe was embarrassed when she was present during the ribbing, but he noticed she said nothing to discourage it.

The nurses and staff must have felt a special sympathy for Joe. Double helpings of his favourite meals and extra ice-cream tubs were to be seen daily on the tray for Patient McCollum. Joe liked seeing his name on the card above his bed, with a Staff Nurse specially assigned to him. He liked too the nurses' easy familiarity with him and their smooth firm arms as they took his blood pressure. How dirty-brown and cracked his arms and hands looked compared to their crisp blue and white uniforms and shining clean skin.

When the Big Doctor came round the ward he was accompanied by a coterie of junior doctors, students and other white-coated attendants.

"This is the man who tried to stop a bus," remarked the Great One, and the group united briefly in a round of discreet professional laughter. "And how are you today, Mr McCollum?"

"I'm grand," Joe managed, just stopping himself from adding 'Your Honour'. "Will I be getting home soon?" he added, as the logical sequel to his own encouraging report.

"I think it's a little early to be thinking of that," smiled the Big Doctor, and his disciples again joined forces in dutiful appreciation of his wit. They passed on to the next patient, leaving Joe proud to be so well known in the highest of places.

By the end of his fourth week in the Male Surgical Ward, Joe was so much into the routine of things that early anxieties about bed baths, bottles and pans were no longer anxieties at all.

It was then that she arrived. Edith Fisher was fully qualified, bristled with certificates, glowed with goodness, and had the delicacy of a sledgehammer. Joe didn't know what a Social Worker was, and felt cowed by her businesslike cheeriness.

"Now, Mr McCollum, we're just going to take a few wee details so that we can be sure what's best for you. It's just a wee chat. We'll take a wee seat here beside your bed and ask you a few wee questions."

Joe was looking for another chair for whoever was with her, but it appeared she was by herself.

The 'few wee questions' lasted half an hour, and covered every aspect of the life and person of Joe McCollum, past and present. The future was saved for another visit. Joe found her questions as uncomfortable as the itching that afflicted his foot below the plaster.

"And how would we manage getting into our wee bath at home with this plaster on?"

"There is no bath. I get washed at the sink."

Edith adjusted her smile and her notes. She did the same on learning that Joe had no inside toilet, but availed of the services offered by a corrugated iron 'wee house' in the back yard.

"And have we central heating? - We have no central heating. And how do we heat our water, have we a wee immersion heater? Oh, we've a wee back boiler. Have we a wee cooked meal every day?"

Joe was trying to give an account of his daily intake and his cooking facilities when she suddenly said 'vegetables'. Not sure if it was an enquiry, an order, or, on her planet, an expletive, Joe gave up on his culinary arrangements and prepared himself for the next attack.

"Now we're going to have to look at your entitlements." Joe was relieved to discover that she was referring only to various benefits and allowances that could be obtained through a maze of forms, booklets, phone calls and agencies. He readily agreed to leave the bookwork to her, happy to fill in Name, Age and Address on a few forms and sign his name in those places she marked with an X. Edith noted down absolutely everything in her plastic-backed folder. He half expected to be asked the width of his leather apron and the number of bootlaces he stocked.

The visits of Edith Fisher became for Joe a series of trials that left him on every occasion weary and unaccountably nervous. Her mouth had a personality of its own, and Joe came to dread the scarlet lipstick and aggressive eyeteeth as he lay watching them at work. It hurt him to hear her describe his home and way of life as '*unfit housing*' and '*below-standard living conditions*'. She explored his financial position - income, expenditure, savings - in a way that reminded him of a taxman who had once called at the shop and subjected him to what could best be described as an interrogation,

Edith wanted to go out to 'assess' Joe's home conditions, but he told her he had dropped his only key in the encounter with the bus.

"Now, we're going to have to think soon about what you're going to do when you leave hospital. They'll soon be wanting your wee bed for somebody else. You won't be able to go home for a wee while, not until that foot's completely better.

Now don't worry, we'll get you into a nice wee convalescent home for a week or two, and take things from there, see how you're getting on, what the doctor says. Have you ever seen inside those lovely wee Folds they have nowadays - really lovely. We could bring you in a wee leaflet or a wee video and you could see for yourself. Believe me, they're the height of luxury..."

I learned all this during my time as chaplain to Silver Lodge Old People's Home, one of the *Happy Hearth Group* of eleven sheltered accommodation Residential Homes for the Elderly. All eleven have disagreeably efficient central heating, and that same unmistakable smell of old age.

I pieced the story together over a number of conversations and cups of tea with a little grey man who joked flatly with the female staff and joined in lifeless banter with the other residents. I noticed that his eyes brightened and his smile came alive only when he was talking about a little brown and black Shoe Repair Shop that reeked of leather and rubber and old-fashioned boot polish.

PATIENCE IS A VIRTUE

Three senseless murders, three women dead, and still no leads, no clues, no witnesses, no suspects. D.I. Moore was feeling the strain as much as the rest of the team, but as Senior Investigating Officer he could sense more keenly the general sense of frustration. He began to hear hopelessness in his colleagues' voices, see it in their faces.

Tuesday evening's incident was evidence of the mood that was taking over. At the end of another day's sterile enquiries Moore had met up with four of the team for a drink at The Mill Pond. They were sitting in their usual corner flatly talking over the dwindling lines of enquiry and the progress, or lack of it, in the investigation of a series of apparently random killings that seemed to have deadened the life of the city.

"OK, the papers are putting the boot in, but forget about them, forget about public opinion, forget everything but the facts, and what are we left looking at? Long hours of stumbling about in the dark and we don't even know if it's a he or a she we're looking for. If we were on 'payment by results' we'd all be in serious trouble with our mortgage repayments." DI Craig lit another cigarette and gulped the smoke down like medicine with the remainder of his pint.

"C'mon, Sam, can you seriously see a woman doing this, killing three other women in cold blood? The shrink's right there at least, our killer is definitely a man."

Their talk was low, earnest, unlike the racket coming from a group of men at the bar. One with a balding head and mousey pigtail must have recognised them. He began to direct his remarks in their direction.

"The police catch him! Don't make me laugh, I've a hack on my lip. The police couldn't catch VD in a brothel."

His mates were sniggering at the witticism when without warning Andrews jumped up and strode round the table, shouting, "I'll put a hack on your lip, you scumbag."

What happened next was straight from a Boys' Own Comic. Sam Craig's perfect rugby tackle brought his colleague down on the dirty tiles, right at the feet of the startled drinkers. The loudmouth was quiet as a statue, and got going again only as Moore was ushering his men out the door and into the street.

Andrews. That was what concerned Moore most. D.S. Andrews was the thoughtful one, the 'steady fellow', the last one likely to detonate. What tensions and pressures were being wound up by the killer out there, and where would he strike again?

Moore poured himself a Johnny Walker Black, dribbled in a little water from the tap, and sat down with the file.

He took a mouthful of the whisky, swilled it round in his mouth, opened the file, and started again into the case of the first victim. The body of Mrs Lorraine Henley had been found by her husband just outside the front door of their Woolner Avenue home. Wilson Henley had come back about nine o'clock from his weekly squash game at Brandon Sports Centre. The lights of his car had picked out his wife's form lying a few feet from the front door. Her bunch of keys was hanging in the lock, her handbag lay a few feet away on the tarmac. At first he thought she had tripped, or taken unwell, but when he saw the blood on the collar of her coat and traced it back to the small hole in her left temple, the case had opened.

As they figured it, the killer had been waiting behind the porch and had stepped round and shot her cleanly in the head as she was reaching to open the door. That meant one of two possibilities. Mrs Henley had been simply a target of opportunity: some marauding nutter had seen her parking her car in the garage and had decided on impulse to kill her. That seemed very unlikely. The more probable scenario was that the killer was someone who knew Lorraine Henley and her routine well enough to plan the shooting, or someone who had watched her over a period of time and timetabled her killing.

Mrs Henley had owned a stationery business left to her by her father. It was a small but successful company with a profitable contract for local government work. Her husband and she had been running the business for twelve years, and had no obvious financial worries. They had no children, no enemies, and, it seemed, no secrets that might account for such a brutal killing.

The crime scene provided no clues at all. Moore skimmed over the facts. The gun used had been a small .25-caliber automatic, a low velocity weapon, light and accessible. There was no exit wound. The powder burns on the skin showed that the shot had been fired at very close range, probably from only a couple of inches. There were no suspicious marks on the body other than the bullet hole. The post mortem examination showed that Mrs Henley had been dead no more than an hour before she was found.

Moore flipped over the technical stuff. It was the bizarre details of the murder that had intrigued him from the start. The killer had carefully arranged the body so that the victim was found lying *with her arms folded*. Equally unusual was what was found in the pocket of her coat. Among the other contents was a playing dice, a red dice on which only the 6 was visible, the yellow dots on the other sides having been painted out. Forensics showed that Cutex nail varnish had been used to erase the numbers. Smudges, and light lines, possibly made by tweezers, ruled out the hope of fingerprints.

As always in such cases, the husband was the first needing to be eliminated from the enquiries. The police investigation into Wilson Henley was sympathetic but thorough. D.I. Craig suspected him from the beginning.

"All right, so his alibi checks out and he's putting up a good show at the grieving husband bit, but you'll find I'm right. There's probably a bit of skirt in this. He's paid somebody to do the job for him. He can easily afford it. All that folded arms and dice nonsense is a smokescreen, decoy stuff."

Moore went along with this as a matter of course, but only to get it off the list. The one thing he trusted, the thing that had propelled him up the ladder to become the youngest Detective Inspector in the Division, was his instinct about people. It was what the older detectives called 'the nose'. Moore could read suspects, could see through the lies of the cleverest of them, their smoothest performances. Equally, he sensed when to believe statements that seemed flawed by inconsistencies or contradictions. In this instance his nose told him that the bewilderment of Mr Henley, his grief, his confusion about certain times and dates and his inaccuracies in some other details, were honest.

Henley was adamant about one thing: Lorraine would not herself have had the dice in her possession. This certainty reinforced Craig's belief that it was a 'plant' that Henley had organised. Moore allowed Craig to keep an eye on Henley, from a distance, especially since there was little else to follow up. The door-to-door enquiries and appeals for witnesses had produced nothing; neighbours and friends were in a state of shocked incredulity and could throw no light at all on her murder. The overall view was that she had been 'a really lovely, quiet person.'

Yes, and what were he and his team of highly trained professionals doing to catch her killer? Moore's mind slid away from the question and back to his childhood. He must have been about thirteen when his uncle was suddenly taken into hospital, and he was charged with helping to look after the small Paint and Wallpaper shop for a week or two. The stultifying boredom of it. Sitting there all day hoping a customer would come in; watching people walking past, mentally urging them to enter; depending entirely upon the public, helpless to influence them. Sometimes a whole day would pass without a single customer opening the shop door. For the first time in his young life Simon Moore had thought about the terrible dreariness of some adults' lives. As early as a boy just into his teens he determined never to be trapped in a job like that. Perhaps that was a factor in his choosing a career in the police.

Yet what was he doing right now? Sitting and hoping for some 'passer-by on the street' to come into his cop shop with a piece of information to restart an investigation that had come to a total halt, a dead-end. Worse, an investigation that had never got off the ground. Moore forced himself back to the job in hand. At a time when his mind needed to be at its sharpest, he couldn't allow it to take trips down the side streets of his past.

"He's telling us he's thrown his six, he's got started," he'd said at the first briefing of the team he had assembled, "so the game's only got under way. We have to assume there'll be more killings."

"Are we sure it's a man, sir?" DS Cooper developed her question. "I mean, there's the nail varnish. And then the gun. It's the kind some women might keep for self-protection, legally or not. Maybe it's another woman, a rival."

As for the folded arms, Meadows, the forensic psychiatrist, had mixed ideas. "The killer may be reaching back to a female authority figure, perhaps a mother or stepmother, a teacher or instructor of some kind. A dominatrix, if there had been sexual abuse, but I rather doubt this. It's a bit of a stereotype, the stern matron type with the folded arms. I'd think it improbable that someone would connect experiences of personal abuse to that popular representation.

On the other hand, the folded arms can represent, not the perpetrator of domination, but its victims, as in the child made to sit with arms folded as a mark of obedience. The murderer may have had sexual failures or humiliation, for example, and may want to deny or counteract these experiences by inflicting total submission and obedience upon women he sees as occupying power or position. The victim in this case would be just such a woman, wealthy, independent, socially, and perhaps therefore for him, sexually, superior.

The odd thing, though, is the suddenness of the death. These people usually want some kind of acknowledgement or recognition from the victim, some kind of relationship almost. Serial killers choose victims they can control or dominate. Simply shooting the victim in the head, as seems to have been the case here, would give the killer no satisfaction. The normal motivation for a crime like this is usually robbery, or revenge, neither of which seems to fit here."

Moore had questioned Mrs Henley's employees and former employees, but drew a blank. Craig's pursuit of her husband led nowhere. Visits to gun dealers and to various cosmetics outlets were merely routine. The trail grew thinner and thinner.

Without saying so to each other, the police were simply marking time until the next killing. The expert's view was that psychotic killers acted in homicidal cycles, and there would probably be an interval of about two months.

The whiskey was burning in his belly. Why was he unable to enjoy something he really enjoyed? Moore reached for the Rennies and moved on to the murder of Linda Devoto.

The criminal psychologist had got his timing wrong. The body of Mrs Devoto was found one month after the first murder, and, as it emerged, that interval was a calculated one. Moore read over the statements and reports he now knew almost off by heart. The killing was identical to the first one except that it took place in broad daylight. Mrs Devoto had been tending the grave of her father, something she did every Friday afternoon, at the old end of the Municipal Cemetery. It appeared that the killer had simply walked up to her as she knelt to place a bunch of flowers and shot her in the side of the head. He may have been in wait for her behind the large old yew tree that shadowed that corner of the graveyard. Moore went through the statement of the council employee who had found her lying half across the grave with her arms folded, like one of the stone or marble figures that adorned some of the larger tombs.

The number left on the dice in her pocket was 4. It was D.S. Andrews who saw its significance: it was four weeks to the day since the death of Mrs Henley. Was the killer throwing a dice to schedule the murders, and if that were so, how could he target his victims successfully.

Moore finished his whiskey and poured himself another, this time omitting the water. He'd pay for it shortly with bitter acid reflux and incineration of his stomach lining, but what the hell, pleasure and pain, pain and pleasure, weren't they always bedfellows in one way or another. In any case, he almost welcomed the burning. Why should he deserve enjoyment when he wasn't doing his job right?

Nobody had heard the shot, nobody had seen anything or anybody suspicious. As for Antonio Devoto, he was inconsolable, frantic in his grief. Even Craig felt bad questioning him about where he had been at the time of the killing, especially when it was established beyond any doubt at all that he had been working in the small prosthetics factory that had come to him like a kind of dowry when he had married Linda.

"There's a connection there," Moore had noted. "Both women were the bosses, the president of the board, so to speak. The killings aren't so random after all. Our man has maybe a whole shopping list of suitable targets, and plans to time their deaths according to the throw of the dice. I'll run it past Meadows and see what he thinks."

"And I'll check what Henley was doing at the time of the murder," growled Craig, who seemed unhappy to let go of his original suspect. "Maybe this second one is to throw us off the scent."

Meadows was uncomfortable with developments. "Fine, the dice could be his way of taunting the police, showing them it's a game he's playing and everything is loaded in his favour. It's odd, just the same, for two reasons. Why is he indicating the day of the killing *after* it has been carried out?

You might have expected the dice to be sent by mail or some other means *before* the killing, as a challenge to the police. These people take meticulous care to avoid detection, but at the same time many of them need the satisfaction that provoking the police gives them. That element of danger and defiance underlines their cleverness, their superiority.

The second thing that puzzles me here is why he should choose something as uncontrolled and unpredictable as the throw of a dice. The serial killer has to believe that he is in total control, not subject to the chance result of any gamble, whether he throws the dice or not.

As for the victims having had positions of power and control in their business and possibly marital relationships, I've met the full range of the downtrodden male, from the common henpecked husband right up to the entrenched misogynist, but none of them with sociopathic tendencies deep enough to make them serial killers. Even if such were the case, our man would need his victims to see and suffer their loss of control, and his domination. An instant bullet in the brain would do nothing to meet the needs of such a psychotic personality."

Moore rubbed his eyes and stretched. He thought over what Meadows had said. It had occurred to him too that a dice was an unusual means for a methodical killer to choose to programme his work. Methodical, even fastidious. The nail varnish had been chosen from a range of brands and shades to match exactly the red of the dice. Then the killings themselves. They were more like professional hits, assassinations carried out by a contract hitman, than the compulsive or obsessive actions of a deranged psychopathic killer.

A whiff of sweat reached him. Another shirt to add to the pile in the basket. Fortunately tomorrow was Thursday and Mrs Davey would be in. Suddenly tiredness set in. He wouldn't read the file on Wendy Barrett, he'd been through it often enough.

But he did go through it once more, in the busy brain that denied him the rest his body craved. 5 on the dice this time, the victim's bare arms folded peacefully in death on the sun lounger, the murder as motiveless and baffling as the others.

The killer had put a bullet in the head of Mrs Barrett as she lay sunbathing in the back garden of her Green Park Court home. She had probably fallen asleep in the heat, allowing her killer to approach and fire at point blank range, but how had he known she was there, and how long had he waited and watched for his opportunity?

As with the first two victims, Mrs Barrett had been a woman of independent means, running a private Employment Agency. Her husband, who found her when he came home from work early in the afternoon after she had failed to answer his series of calls to her mobile, was, if anything, in even greater distress than Henley or Devoto had been, and had to be sedated by the scene of crime medical officer.

For a time they had seemed to have a lead. Neighbours had seen a dark blue or black car, possibly a Citroen, cruising up and down the broad leafy avenue, and a man who had been working in one of the laundered gardens had got a good look at the driver. There was a buzz among the team in the Incident Room, a feeling that finally they had something to follow up. Car dealers, garages, licensing authorities and private motor clubs were contacted and an appeal was made to the public. Hopes died as quickly as they had arisen when the driver turned up at his local police station and identified himself as a financial advisor on a home call looking for the house number of a new client. The client quickly verified his story.

Three meaningless killings. Three women from different parts of the city, all married, middle aged, successful, apparently happy. None had children, in each case by choice. Meadows regarded this latter fact as of possible assistance in his attempts to build some kind of profile of a serial killer who, in his words, 'broke all the rules'.

Moore adjusted his pillow and focused his thoughts on forming an overview of the criminal and the crimes. This was no longer a random psychopathic killer but an extremely organised one, somebody capable of selecting and targeting a particular type of victim, somebody with the time, means and mobility to carry out his work across the city without leaving one clue or making one mistake. Was he unemployed, perhaps unmarried, to have the opportunities to stalk and label his targets. Moore was certain that each murder was carefully set up, perhaps even rehearsed, which involved a long period of learning the victims' routines and daily programmes. The team had already checked deliverymen, service men, repairmen, anyone who might have had some connection with the three murder victims, but had drawn a blank.

When Moore woke at six the next morning his mind went instantly back to work, trying in something close to desperation to get a toehold on the mountain of glass that the case had become.

"I knew there was something wrong when the oven buzzed and she wasn't back. She's always back before it buzzes. She's never been back too late for the oven buzzing."

The man was clearly in shock. His mind had stuck at that point; the only thing out of order was his wife's uncharacteristic failure to get back in time, even though he had found her lying, arms folded and with a bullet hole in her head, five minutes' walk away. He had wandered into the house next door and told them what had happened and that the timer on the oven was buzzing.

The murder scene was the rural equivalent of an alleyway, a lane that ran along the bottom of the back gardens of an avenue of well appointed suburban houses bordered by the outer reaches of a golf course. The laneway was cordoned off and a small tent had been erected. Moore knew that somewhere on the body, probably in the pocket of the cream cardigan, there would be a red dice reading only a 2.

D.S. Cooper had got hold of the dead woman's little Scottie and was soothing its whimpering. Moore and she left the pathologist and forensic team to their business and walked back to the house to try to piece together from Mr Warburton and his neighbour the circumstances of the killing.

There wasn't much that promised to be helpful. Apparently the deceased was a lady of strict habit.

"You could set your watch by Anna Warburton," the neighbour said in sad admiration. Each evening when she returned from work she would prepare the meal and place it in the oven with the timer precisely set. She would then take Chippy for his daily walk round part of the rim of the golf course, timing her return to beat the oven by a few minutes. Her husband's duty was to set the table and try to catch the sports section of the TV news.

"She's never back late. That's how I knew something wasn't right. It went on and on buzzing. I didn't know how to stop it, so I went looking for her. That's when I found her, when I went to get the buzzing stopped." Mr Warburton didn't want to go beyond that point, and it was the neighbour who finished the story. It was he who had phoned the police when 'John was at the door saying his wife was dead and the oven was buzzing.'

Predictably nobody had heard the shot, nobody had seen any suspicious characters or activity. It was the time of day when people in a district like Oakwood were inside having their evening meal and watching the news. Moore had the entire area, including the golf course, sealed off, but turned up nothing. The pathologist's on-site report simply confirmed what they already knew or presumed, and beyond corroborating the number on the dice, forensics could find nothing of worth. The body of Mrs Anna Warburton was removed for a full post mortem examination. Mr Warburton's doctor, after giving him a strong sedative, ruled his patient not fit for further questioning that evening.

Except that the victim was in her late fifties, the Warburton killing was a perfect match for the others. She was a Polish woman who had met John Warburton literally by accident when he was a young man in her country alone on an angling vacation. She had been the only nurse in the small hospital who spoke any English when he arrived with the broken wrist that had cut short his fishing holiday. A year's correspondence and one visit each way later and they were man and wife. The marriage had produced no children.

Like the others, Anna Warburton had been a successful and enterprising woman. She had run a small chain of Health Food shops, and advised on healing methods and treatments such as reflexology, aromatherapy and acupuncture. John helped behind the counter, or made collections and deliveries.

Moore made a mental note to check if any of the first three victims had availed of these services, and arranged for home deliveries over the past year to be examined, but didn't expect to find any connection. His nose had already told him that his time spent with Warburton was only for the formbook.

Craig was there if any sweet and sour was needed. Moore nodded him into the background. They were in the stiffly furnished front room, light filtering through the slatted blinds. Warburton seemed to have aged, his shoulders rounded as if the weight of the realisation of what had happened the previous evening was a physical one. He was a wispy man in his late forties. Moore noted absently that he had married an older woman. He wondered idly if the marriage certificate had been for Anna no more than a passport or work permit.

It was clear that the man was more concerned about himself than about the death of his wife or the identity of her killer. "What am I going to do? I can't run the business on my own, I left all that to Anna. I'll have to sell it, I'll never be able to cope by myself. How could I manage it, I couldn't handle things on my own. You can't expect me to take all that on."

The tone was self-pitying, almost petulant, with none of the grief the other bereaved husbands had shown. Craig caught Moore's eye and raised an eyebrow, but

Moore shook his head. Nothing suspicious, the natural anxieties of a weak swimmer facing deep water. For some people the how and why questions about a murder were things that came later, only after they had settled in their minds its effects upon themselves. Moore had seen this many times before. True, Warburton fitted the profile of the male in a subordinate position to his wife, but then, to varying degrees, so did the husbands of the three other victims.

Moore avoided the inane questions that were almost written into the murder detective's script. He had never been given the name of someone who might have wanted to harm the victim, nor had witnesses ever been able to remember where they had been on the dates of previous incidents. The average person didn't know today's date, or remember what he was doing two nights ago.

"No luck with the fishing, then? I don't see the pictures on the wall with you holding up the catch of the day. I thought every angler had at least one of those up on display?" Worthington gave a sad, shy little smile. "Gave it up years ago. Haven't the time."
Moore nodded sympathetically and asked a few more questions about Anna's friends and employees. Suddenly he darted, "And do you tie your own flies?"
Worthington looked up with surprise and interest. "No, I didn't. Do you? Are you an angler?"

"What was that fishing thing about, sir? D'you like him?"
Craig was a good detective, but he watched too much NYPD. "I love him," said Moore savagely. "Turn the car and go back, I forgot to give him a kiss."

The needle daubed red varnish over the head of the fly. It was a Thunderflash he had tied. He waited for the varnish to dry. It took a little longer than nail varnish.

He unclamped the fly from the vice, and put in another size 8 double hook. That had been a 'dicey' moment when the big one in the dark suit had thrown the fly-tying question. He laughed at his little joke, and chose a pinch of yellowcrest feather to tie in at the tail.

It was two weeks since the funeral. He'd 'throw' another four. It would look better, more convincing, if the same number came up twice. He didn't really want to kill a fifth one now that he'd got Anna over and done with, the job completed, but it might draw attention to him if the killings stopped with her. No, he'd do just one more. The Mylar body was neat; he'd wind a rib of oval gold tinsel and use some yellow beard hackle for the throat. Lovely.

Patience. It was all about patience. He was a born angler, a man of patience. What had he to do with herbs and treatments and appointments and deliveries and remedies? Why should he have to use up his life on Anna and her worried, wrinkled women? No doubt he could expect some further police attention, they'd go on looking for their serial killer, not knowing the real work was over. They'd never appreciate the years of patience needed, the care he had taken to make sure there were no children involved. Yes, it had taken a real angler's time and patience to find the ones with no children, but it was worth it. It would have spoiled everything if he'd felt guilty over a child having to suffer the way he had suffered.

A length of black squirrel for the overwing and a couple of strands of Flashabou next. Warburton rubbed his hands in satisfaction. All he'd ever really wanted was now his but, patience, he'd wait a year or so. They might be watching him, or wanting to keep him informed. Then he'd start with the salmon season in Russia. The Kola Peninsula trip, fishing the Kharlovka, the Eastern Litza, the Rynda. After that, probably Alaska, Prince William Sound.

Now just the build up of the tidy head secured with whip finish and the joy of the red varnish. He finished the fly with patient pleasure, folded his arms, and allowed himself another little laugh.

MITZI

Even another cat lover could hardly have appreciated her grief, so why would she expect him to understand it? Him. She'd done it again. At the beginning her husband in Clare's mind had always been Jackie, but recently, and especially since Mitzi's disappearance, she found herself repeatedly thinking in terms of 'he' and 'him'. It reminded her uncomfortably of her former boss who never referred to his wife by name, but always as her: *I have to pick her up after work today* or *Ring her and tell her I'll be home late this evening.* Clare put the thought to one side and allowed her sorrow to replay the events leading to the loss of her lovely little black and white longhaired cat.

She had sensed from the start that Mitzi was not coming back, had felt it inside from teatime on Tuesday when she hadn't appeared. Normally she would insinuate herself through the cat-flap, devour the food left in her dish, stretch, yawn, and jump up on Clare's lap for a purr and a prolonged head massage. Clare loved how Mitzi would butt her little head into her hand if the stroking stopped. Her eyes filled up again at the memory.

As the hours passed and her anxiety deepened Jackie had made all the right noises, discounting her fears and offering favourable explanations for Mitzi's absence.

"There's nothing to worry about. Cats do this every so often; nobody knows where they go off to or why, but they always come back again. They know where they're well looked after."

Clare noticed that even by ten o'clock, when the situation had become really alarming, he was still sneaking glances past her at extra time being played in yet another stupid football match. In light of what was to follow his words now seemed cold, hollow, almost corrupt: "Go out and look for her? Are you serious? At this time of night? And where would we start? I tell you, cats are their own bosses. She'll be back in her own good time, she'll be here in the morning."

Clare shuddered at how empty his assurances had proved to be. Even the way he used the word 'cats' upset her, as if he saw Mitzi as only that, a cat, a creature, not the warm fluffy little pet that had first choice of chair in the evening and slept on their bed at night. Yes, and in cold weather, in the bed. Let others laugh or condemn, but Clare missed Mitzi like she would have missed a child. She remembered her friend Julie's words after the tragic cot death of her little boy: *how will I ever forget him when my own life every day is a constant reminder?*

Well, soppy or not, that was how she would always remember Mitzi. She didn't care if 'sensible' people would think her soft in the head. Better that than being like the utterly hateful woman next door, the one who claimed to be an animal lover. When Jackie and she had knocked late that evening and asked about Mitzi, all they got was a terrifying account of the ferocity of her Jack Russell.

"I hope for her sake that cat of yours didn't come over here. This fellow's a lamb with me, but let anyone or anything else near him, and he can be a very nasty little piece of homework. He saw off a Kerry Blue the other week and..."

Clare didn't sleep a wink that night. They had made a few enquiries at neighbouring houses and informed the police, but Jackie was half-hearted about the whole thing. He made her ring the police station, and insisted she came to bed instead of sitting up waiting. For all his declared interest and concern, he was in deep sleep inside a few minutes.

Next morning, unbelievably, he was all set to go to work as usual, and only after desperate pleading had she been able to persuade him to help her look for the still missing Mitzi. That moment when they found her mangled remains crushed beside the kerbside would never leave her.

It was Jackie who spotted her first. He stopped some distance away and made Clare stay in the car. Without a box or blanket to carry her, he lifted her carefully and brought her back to the boot of the car. Clare noticed him checking his shirtfront and cuffs for bloodstains.

Did he have to use the word 'flattened', however accurate it might have been? The thought of someone doing that to poor little Mitzi and then driving on, leaving her lying there, her lovely little face squashed to a bloody mess for flies and magpies, was enough to make Clare nearly sick.

She sobbed all the way home. Part of her wanted to see Mitzi for the last time, but Jackie stopped her. "We'll take her down to Bert's farm and give her a nice burial down there. It'll be better, Clare, if you remember her that way. If we bury her here she'll be too close to you."

How had she allowed herself to be talked into agreeing to that? What did Jackie's brother Bert have to do with it? He'd never even seen Mitzi. Yet her lovely little pet had been taken away down there to an unknown place, miles from the avenue and home and garden she had loved to play in every day. A shuddering truth struck her. It wasn't her feelings Jackie had been so tender about, it was his garden - he didn't want to dig a hole in his precious garden.

Suddenly all was clear; through eyes brimming with tears all was clear, cruelly clear. She didn't love him, not now, probably not ever. She didn't even like him. Mitzi's death had led her to acknowledge what she had known but refused to recognise the whole two and a half years of their marriage - he was a selfish pig, a cold-hearted brute. Her marriage was a lie. For the second night in succession Clare went without sleep.

Jackie took her in a cup of tea and a biscuit. What was that sinking feeling he got now every time he saw her, that need for space, to be free, to be at the club or park enjoying male pursuits? The frilliness of Clare's whole person and being was now something that irritated him more than he could ever explain, even to himself. The whole Mitzi business was a kind of symbol for it. Mitzi - wasn't the name just typical. Imagine telling his mates at the club that he had been out knocking doors and making funeral arrangements for his little cat Mitzi.

He recalled a moment in the vet's clinic: a tough-looking type had come into the waiting room, his tattooed arms cradling a sick hamster. Asked by the receptionist for the hamster's name he had shyly replied *Margaret*, and a Mexican wave of subdued laughter had gone round the waiting room. That's what Jackie could expect at the football club, minus the subdued part. Yet 'mitziness' was the quality Clare wanted in him, the quality she could always find to admire in her friends' husbands.

"Here's a cup of tea, Clare. It'll make you feel better."

"It'll what? You have it yourself, your feelings aren't too hard to lift."

Jackie felt a surge of instant anger. "Oh, right, sorry, I forgot - you're the only one allowed to have feelings in this house. That's the way you like it, isn't it? Me the ogre so that you can have all the sympathy. Well, I have my own feelings. Just because I don't burst into tears and sit shaking all day, with nothing else to do, doesn't mean I don't feel things just as much as you do."

Jackie was enjoying the offensive, and her defiant silence drove him on. "I can't sit all day feeling sorry for myself, I've a job to go to, and money to earn to let you buy your swags and tails and your frilly cushion covers."

The tea was sloshing over the cup into the saucer from the vehemence of Jackie's delivery. He set them down to resume the onslaught. "It's always been the same with you. When something goes wrong you need somebody to blame, a target, and it's never yourself. I have to be the enemy, as if that does any good. Blaming me won't bring Mitzi back. You should be thanking me. Who's the one searched through that building site, wheelbarrows, cement mixers and all, getting dirty looks from the workers? And who had to find a shoebox while you sat sniffling, absolutely useless. And all that fuss about finding Mitzi's favourite ball to put in it, and that stupid wind-up mouse, and cutting flowers from my garden, what did all that prove?"

Clare looked up at him with an expression of pure distaste and turned the back of her carefully waved hair to him. Jackie sensed that she was winning the argument, in spite of his best rhetoric, and went straight to the finale. "I'll tell you something else. I don't care, I don't give a shit, what you think, so think whatever you like."

He would have said more but knew he had given it his best shot. He left for the club, heightening the effect in his judgement by banging the door behind him.

It was about half nine and Clare was in the kitchen, free of Jackie's presence but weighed down by heavier matters, when she heard, or perhaps sensed, something at the window. She glanced up. The shape outside stopped her heart and sent a chill right through her. Standing on the sill, its front paws pressed high against the glass, was the ghost of her beloved Mitzi. Clare's head reeled, she closed her eyes in horror, felt faint, but couldn't stop herself looking again. The image was gone.

She doesn't remember opening the back door, but next thing she was outside on the patio and something was rubbing round her ankles. Clare bent down out of habit and felt a familiar furry head butting into the palm of her hand. For a few delirious moments her joy was complete until the terrible thought came that took her breath away and made her weak at the knees - someone was probably out there looking for a little black and white cat that was buried in a shoebox down in the country on her brother-in-law Bert's farm..........

THE DUFFLE COAT MAN

The police station smelt of sweat and polished wood, like a school gym. The woman made her way to the counter, her husband sullen behind her. The Desk Sergeant had that petty official's habit of needing to finish writing before he could attend to her. She could sense her husband bristling at her side.

"Good afternoon, madam." It was a question.

"I want to make a complaint about somebody, a man who's pestering me."

"Good enough. Hold on." He spoke over her shoulder. "Gil, have you a minute?" A round-shouldered man in a light gray suit was passing. He paused. "This lady wants to see you."

"Wants to see me? Me in particular?" The man peered at her, looking not too pleased.

"Sorry, Gil, but there's no uniforms about, and I've all these reports to tidy up...."

Gil hesitated, as if about to move on, but then abruptly closed the file he was carrying and set it on the counter. He looked tired and overworked.

"C'mon, Anna, they're too busy, they've more important things to do." Her husband's voice was brittle with anger.

Gil glanced at him, ignored him, and said to Anna, "Sorry, it's one of those days. What do you want to see me about?"

He introduced himself as D.C. Meldrum. Anna had imagined a meeting with a detective would have been in a separate room, with a desk between them, as in T.V. police dramas, but they were merely sitting on two shabby chairs in a corner of the main entrance lobby, with her husband hovering a few yards away, ready for affront. She gave the detective her name and address, adding, "This is my husband, Brian," but neither man acknowledged the other.

The detective studied her. She was a well-dressed woman in her mid thirties, with middle age not yet marking out its intentions, or perhaps carefully hidden under the generous makeup. Not immediately pretty, he thought, but attractive with the kind of attractiveness that grew the longer he looked at her, especially in the fine mouth that formed its words effortlessly.

Anna made her complaint without interruption. Meldrum seemed to be hardly listening, but every so often he would suddenly dart a penetrating look at her, before going back to twiddling the ring on his hairy wedding finger. It was a bit disconcerting.

"About six weeks or so ago this man started talking to me after I came out of Coburn Green Underground. I was walking towards the subway up to Epson Street." She paused. Meldrum nodded to show he knew the place. She gave brief details of her job, working hours and journey times, and Meldrum again nodded, to show he had absorbed the information.

"At first I thought he was maybe a bit simple or something, because he wasn't drunk and didn't look like a down-and-outer, but it soon became clear that he was sensible enough. I mean, he wasn't talking nonsense or anything like that, he was just, how would you put it, making conversation with me, keeping me company through the underpass. I made a few polite replies the first time, but when he was there again the next evening I just walked on, saying nothing. Then he appeared again, and again, always in the same place and talking to me.

What started to worry me was that I seemed to be the only one he was talking to. You maybe know yourself that it's an empty place near the end of the Outer Line, but even when there were other people walking through, other women, and girls, he never bothered with them. He wasn't there every evening, maybe two or three times a week. Sometimes he'd suddenly appear from nowhere and sometimes he was standing inside the tunnel, as if he was waiting for me.

I started getting nervous about it, never knowing if he was going to be there or not, and hoping he wouldn't be. I wasn't afraid of him, not exactly, just uncomfortable."

During her narration Brian was impatiently toeing the skirting board, like a child sworn to good behaviour but bursting for activity. Anna paused, but the detective waited for her to continue.

"Well, it's still going on, and I've reached the stage that I hate walking through that tunnel. A few evenings I came home from work by bus to miss it out, but the bus service is so slow and poor that it's not an option. Brian picked me up a few times, but of course the man didn't appear those evenings. Brian's job is on the east side, and he doesn't finish in time to meet me regularly, and he can't get out of work early every evening."

"You needn't make excuses for me." Brian's vow of silence had broken. "It's not my fault this is still happening. Get me on your mobile, and if this guy likes talking, keep him talking until I get there, and I'll soon put the talking out of him. Anyway, what do the police care? They're probably checking if we've parked on a double yellow line. I've told you a hundred times, I'll sort this out for you. Just you get me on the mobile and I'll soon sort this scummer out."

Anna sighed. What was the point in trying to reason with him? Meldrum waited until he was sure she had nothing further to add.

"When was the last time this man appeared, Mrs Young?"

"Yesterday evening. Friday."

"You'll be able to describe him?"

"Only too well. He's white, in his forties, I'd say, about the same size and build as my husband, but a bit heavier. He's got grayish black hair and a moustache the same. He always wears one of those dark brown duffle coat things, with the hood up."

"How can you be sure of his hair if he wears the hood up?" shot Meldrum suddenly, that look catching her again.

"It's long at the sides. I don't mean hippy long or anything like that, it's just that you can see his hair clearly inside the hood. I never look at him when he's walking along talking beside me, but I'd recognise him anywhere."

Meldrum seemed satisfied, and asked a few more questions about appearance, accent, distinguishing marks. "What exactly does he talk to you about, Mrs Young?"

"That's just it, nothing really. Ordinary things like the weather, traffic, litter, prices, nothing special, as if he enjoys the talking part, no matter what it's about."

"Has he ever said anything of a personal or sexual nature to you?"

"Never."

"Has he ever threatened you, or got angry, or been offensive or objectionable in any way?"

"No, I don't think so. I'm not listening most of the time, I'm just trying to get away from him. I just can't stand him so close to me, and talking to me as if he knew me, or I knew him. It's really getting to me."

"Has he tried to follow you?"

"No. As I said, he's just there, sometimes outside the subway, sometimes inside it. He never goes on through into Epson Street. I don't know where he goes, or what he does. He tells me he likes talking to me, even though I ignore him and don't say a word in reply."

"Has he ever touched you, or made any kind of physical contact?"

"No. He just walks along beside me, as if we were friends."

"Have you told him to leave you alone, or have you threatened him with the police if he doesn't stop bothering you?"

"No, I don't say anything. I just want him to get out of my life."

"Have you thought about coming home at a different time, or by a different route?"

"Why should she? Why should she? Why should she upset her whole routine because of some scumbag? That's just typical of you people, don't worry about the victim, and don't upset the criminal." Brian was spitting with anger.

Meldrum ignored him. "And you say you're not afraid of this man, Mrs Young? You don't think he might harm you in some way?"

"No. Yes. I don't know. I just don't want him waiting for me, watching for me, walking and talking with me."

"Why didn't you find a policeman in the street and go back and get this man cautioned for bothering you?"

"I thought about that, but by the time I would have found a policeman and gone back he'd probably have been away."

Meldrum said nothing for a minute or so, as if trying to arrive at the best way to give unwelcome news.

"Well, strictly speaking, Mrs Young, this is not really a matter for me at all. We're paid to investigate crimes. There's no crime here, and no suggestion that a crime is going to be committed. It seems the worst this man is, in the eyes of the law, is a kind of nuisance, and not a very bad one at that. He's not exactly stalking you, he isn't molesting or threatening you, he's not being offensive, and there's no law against him talking to you. We can't charge a man for what he might do, and in your case it doesn't seem as if this man wants to do anything more than talk. The best I could do would be to send a constable down to have a word with him, but, as you say yourself, it's hit and miss, and I can't afford to send an officer down regularly to look for a man who's maybe just lonely and wanting a few minutes' harmless talk."

The detective may well have added a few words of apology or understanding, but he didn't get the chance.

"What did I tell you?" Brian exploded. "Useless, totally useless, a complete waste of time. Let the thugs and the scumbags do what they like, let them rob and rape and intimidate, and then lift your big salary at the end of the month. Aye, it's a hard life being a policeman. C'mon, Anna, I'll deal with this my own way, like I told you from the start."

She tried to protest, but Young urged her off the chair and ushered her towards the door, his face red with rage. Meldrum didn't move, but called after him, "I'd watch that temper of yours, sir. It could get you into serious trouble."

By the time Meldrum reached the subway it had been sealed off with blue and white tape. He nodded to the young officer, ducked under the tape, and headed for the small group a hundred yards inside. The tunnel stank of urine, and its dim overhead lighting only half lit the graffiti-scrawled walls.

The body of Brian Young lay face down, close to the left wall. A mess of blood had leaked from the head. A police photographer was at work, together with the other scene of crime regulars. Some distance away a woman constable was comforting the victim's wife, whose face looked yellowish in the weak bulkhead lighting. Under the drab arch of the tunnel she seemed to Meldrum smaller than the woman he had spoken to in the police station ten days earlier.

"Any witnesses?" he asked the young officer, who had arrived at the scene only minutes after the killing.

"The victim's wife, sir, and the girl who came on the scene and ran back and got me. I was only a few hundred yards up Epson Street. She says all she saw was the body lying on the floor and the woman standing screaming. There's a couple of witnesses saw the man hurrying towards the Underground. Not much help. He had a hooded jacket or something on, and they just thought it was somebody rushing for a train. We're trying to reach people who were in the station or using the line."

At that moment the forensics arrived. Meldrum didn't like the pathologist, so he merely nodded, planning to talk to him when he'd finished his examination. The detective watched for a minute or two as the body was carefully turned over.

Anna Young stood unmoving, staring at nothing. Meldrum drew the WPC aside for a brief word.

"I think she's badly shocked, sir, but you can talk to her all right. She seems to be blaming herself for this."

Meldrum adjusted his tone. "I'm very sorry about what has happened, Mrs Young." She looked at him slowly, but didn't reply. "I'm going to have to ask you a few questions, I'm afraid." She nodded. " Can you tell me what happened? Did you see the man who did this?"

Anna turned towards him, her face heavy with defeat. "I should never have agreed to it. I told him to stay out of it, but he kept on and on, on and on, wearing me down, wanting to prove something, to himself, or to me, or whatever, and look what's happened." She paused. "He made a terrible, funny little noise, like a gurgle or something. I can still hear it." She shuddered and crouched into herself, like a child trying to keep warm.

Meldrum expertly prised the facts from her. She had been bullied by her husband into his plan of action to 'sort things out'. Brian's boss had agreed that for two weeks he could work during his lunch hour and finish early. He had met Anna coming out of work each evening and they had taken the Underground together to Coburn Green station. Anna had then walked ahead, with her husband following a short distance behind.

"For nearly a whole week he didn't show, and I thought maybe it was all over."

Anna stopped and reached into her bag for her cigarettes. Her fingers were trembling. Meldrum gave her a light. He lit one of his own.

"He was standing just over there, kind of huddled into the wall, his back half turned and his face hidden in the hood. I didn't need to tell Brian, he saw him right away. He rushed past me and the man turned round and... and then...there was a funny kind of ...of dancing.... and Brian crumpled to the ground making this noise in his throat...and the man walked straight past me.... and I went over and there was blood coming out below Brian's head... I could see it spilling out...and there was a noise going on inside my head, and I realised it was me screaming." She put her hands to her throat, as if to stop the bleeding, and swayed so badly that Meldrum had to steady her. He gave orders for the policewoman to have her looked after and taken home.

The on site forensic report was brutally simple. Death had occurred as a result of two deep wounds to the throat produced by a long, sharp instrument such as a kitchen knife. The wounds suggested that the blows were thrusts into the throat rather than downward stabbings. In the words of the forensic man, the murder had been 'a good job'.

"A mug of coffee'll be fine." It was early the following afternoon and Detective Meldrum was in Mrs Young's Ashford Avenue kitchen in the resolutely middle class Cottrell district. He had rung earlier and she had readily agreed that he could come round to 'fill in a few gaps' as the murder enquiry began. Meldrum had brought with him his favourite WPC to help him with 'any woman's stuff'.

Anna looked pale but composed. She showed them into the lounge, inexpensively but tastefully furnished. They talked briefly about how she was bearing up, official identification, and autopsy arrangements.

Meldrum gulped down the last of his coffee, produced the same little red notebook, and set to work. He quickly ascertained that the Youngs had been married for fourteen years and had no children.

"I'm sorry if some of the things I'm asking you might seem to have no bearing on the death of your husband, Mrs Young, but I'm a bit of an old-fashioned plodder. I like to start at the centre and work outwards, so to speak."

"That's fine. Anything. Whatever you think best." The sudden glances were now gone. He kept his eyes fixed on her throughout the meeting.

"What did your husband work at?"

Brian Young had been the buyer and stock controller of a large bed and mattress business in a Retail Park on the east edge of town.

"He hadn't always worked there?" The detective put his question in that statement kind of way that made Mrs Young feel he knew the answer already.

"No, he was a full time instructor for the Sports Council before that." Meldrum frowned for further information. "He had to give that job up." She dropped her eyes.

"An injury?"

She knew, she felt sure, that he knew about Brian's dismissal, but wanted to hear it from her.

She told it all, evenly and squarely, how her husband's temper had lost him the job he loved, how his lack of self-control had 'cost him his career'. He had been coaching a High School class on the sports field. A boy at his elbow had yelled in delight when a schoolmate had cleared the high jump bar, and in an instant rage her husband had cuffed him on the side of the head. The blow had burst the boy's eardrum, and its consequences had stayed with Young every day of his life afterwards. The judge told him he wasn't fit to be in charge of young people, and only his clear record saved him from a prison sentence. On top of the hefty fine, he ordered Brian to attend an Anger Management course.

Anna thought she had finished her reply, but the detective said nothing and looked steadily at her to continue.

"Well, I wish I could say things improved, but. ......Brian hates his work, he's so..." She suddenly remembered, and dropped her head. "I'm sorry, I forgot, he hated..." and she started weeping softly, her dark hair drooping over her deep red fingernails. Meldrum wondered if they had been freshly painted that morning. He waved his cigarettes to WPC Dawson, who collected them, selected her caring voice, and offered one to the silently grieving woman.

"I usually don't smoke in the house, but I suppose these are exceptional circumstances." Anna tried a thin smile through the tears, but gave up on it.

Meldrum allowed a few minutes for Dawson to do her bit, and nodded her back to her place. "Just a couple more questions, Mrs Young. I'm sorry, but I'll be as quick as I can. How well would you say your marriage was going?"

The sudden directness of the question startled her. She looked over to WPC Dawson for support, but found none. The caring bit was over. Again she sensed that the detective was asking for what he already knew.

"Brian was not the man I married, Mr Meldrum. He was different even before he lost his job, moody and bitter, and blaming me because we had no children. When he found out that the problem was his, not mine, he got worse." She hesitated. "I'd asked him for a divorce but he went into a rage and refused point blank. I've been to see a solicitor."

"Why didn't he want you to report this man who's been bothering you?"

"That's Brian. He believes…believed…in nothing or nobody. He said the police couldn't care less, they'd do nothing, they're lazy and interested only in what he called 'soft targets', motorists and the like. He was fined for speeding last year and was in a black mood for weeks after it."

"And did you believe him? About the police?"

"No. That's why I came down to the station last week to make the complaint."

Meldrum considered the reply. He got up and thanked her for her time and help, promising to keep her informed about any progress in catching her husband's killer.

On the doorstep he suddenly asked, "And you're sure you'd be able to recognise the man in the green duffle coat again?"

"It's brown. His coat's brown."

"Oh yes, so it is. Sorry."

The detective was as good as his word. At four the next afternoon Anna got his call.

" Mrs Young? D.C. Meldrum. How are you? Good. Look, there's been an important development here. Could you come down to the station? We need one or two little i's dotted and t's crossed before we can proceed. Would you like us to send a car for you?"

They were in a separate room this time, with a desk between them, and the same WPC hovering in the background. Anna took the chair and the cigarette Meldrum offered her. He was still wearing the same suit. There was a kind of track worn on its breast pocket from daily pen traffic. He sat so far forward, over the desk, that his face was only a few feet from hers.

"Good news, Mrs Young. We've made a breakthrough in our investigation, a real breakthrough." He watched her narrowly. "We're hoping to be in a position to charge somebody very soon."

"Have you got him?" she asked, surprised, her cigarette smoke untidy.

"Let me tell you what I've been up to," the detective said, waving aside the smoke and the question. "When I told you, Mrs Young, that your complaint was not my kind of work, I was telling you the truth. And yet, I was interested. You see, I like puzzles. It's my job to solve puzzles, and there were some puzzles in your story."

He took off his jacket and hung it over his chair. "Let me give you an example: why had you come down to the station to make your complaint, when the obvious and easiest thing to do was to report the man to the nearest policeman? You must have seen one or two every day on Epson Street as you were walking home. Wouldn't that have been the simple thing? Or you could have phoned the station. Or if you wanted to make your complaint in person, wouldn't it have been wiser to come by yourself? Why drag along a husband who was dead set against going to the police, and all too likely to make a scene? Puzzles, Mrs Young, puzzles."

Meldrum stubbed out his cigarette without taking his eyes off her. Her finely formed mouth looked a little slack.

"Let me tell you something this job has taught me, Mrs Young: always be careful of the witnesses who tell it too well, too neat, no mistakes. They're as dodgy as the ones who get nothing right."

"What's all this about?" she broke in. "You're supposed to be on my side, and instead you seem to be playing some kind of game with me." Her voice was shaky.

"OK. I was puzzled enough to go over to Coburn Green myself on Monday to nose around a bit. One of the 'Big Issue' brigade remembered once or twice seeing somebody in a brown duffle coat with the hood up, just like you described, but couldn't remember much, except it was round about 'going home' time. He thinks he saw him talking to a woman a couple of times. The odd thing was that nobody in the station or in Epson Street could remember seeing him. There's a news-stand man on the street catches all the commuters coming and going through that subway, but he'd never seen him. I went over again, twice, just after six, and saw you and your husband, just like you said, but that was it. I questioned one or two six o'clock regulars, but nobody could remember seeing the duffle coat man in the Underground. A few were fairly sure they had seen him a number of times after they came out of the station and were walking the few hundred yards to the subway. Curiouser and curiouser."

The detective paused, looking for comment, but Anna sat silent, staring at the battered tin ashtray.

"Do you know a little Coffee Shop called Delvaro's?" he asked suddenly. She looked up sharply, a flicker of fear on her face, but made no reply. "I didn't know it, not until Wednesday past. It's one of those 'little out-of-the-way places', where people can meet in private. Let me tell you how I came upon it.

I hope I'm not boring you, Mrs Young. My wife tells me I'm a bore. Once I get onto a subject, I keep on and on, even when nobody else is interested. That's the way I was with you and this man in the brown duffle coat. I wanted to know more. That's why I called round to your work the following day. That would have been Wednesday. As luck would have it, you were just coming out of the front entrance. Must have been your lunch hour.

Now why did I start following you? Maybe this job gives a man bad habits. Anyway, that's how I found Delvaro's, tucked away down Mariner's Entry, and saw that nice young man you were talking to so seriously over your coffee.

You know, if I hadn't known you to be a married woman, I might have thought he was your lover. That's the kind of bad mind I have. And why did I desert you, and follow him when he came out of the Coffee Shop a few minutes after you? Very ungallant. My wife's right, I'll never make a gentleman. And why did I take the same bus right out to Bailmill Estate, and make a note of where he lived?"

Anna Young's expression had changed from fear to hatred as Meldrum toyed with her.

"All right, so you were having an affair. Couldn't say I was surprised. I still wanted to know more about the duffle coat man, but, pressure of work, I had to put him to one side. That is, of course, until the murder of your husband put him right back to the head of the queue."

Meldrum reached down into his jacket pocket and produced his cigarettes. He took one for himself and set the packet down on the desk between them. Anna ignored them. He was pleased.

"So there we were, with a murder, and a suspect even before it happened," he continued. "Nice. Except, I knew all about the victim and precious little about the suspect. Who was he, this mysterious duffle coat man? Where was he? Further enquiries produced the same results: several people remembered seeing the man in the brown duffle coat at the same time of day, in the same place, that dark stretch of walkway between the steps down from the Coburn Green Underground and the pedestrian subway, and in the subway itself. One witness is sure she saw him with a woman, talking to her. Nobody, apart from yourself, however, had any recollection of his face or any other features. If only he hadn't worn that hood up."

Meldrum paused again. Office noises of printers and fax machines could be heard from somewhere in the building, but the silence in the room was total.

"How did we get him, Mrs Young? We've had him now in custody for 24 hours, and we're about to charge him with the murder of your husband once those dots and crosses are sorted out."

She hadn't said a word throughout Meldrum's recital, the pretty mouth tightened into a grim line.

They had examined the Underground CCTV tapes from the previous six weeks. No hooded figure in a duffle coat appeared on any of them. What did interest the team of detectives was the behaviour of a young man carrying a sports bag. On a number of occasions, just before six in the evening, he got off at Coburn Green, only to reappear fifteen minutes or so later on the other platform to take a train in the return direction.

"Now where had I seen him before? Surely it couldn't be that nice young man I'd seen talking to the victim's poor wife in a discreet little Coffee Shop down town."

"He was there looking after me," she screamed, "trying to protect me. He loves me, and I love him. Don't you dare make little of him, you bastard. He loves me."

"Don't bother, Mrs Young. Oh yes, you were smart, all right. A character that people remembered, but not clearly. From your account, eccentric and, who knows, maybe liable to violence. A victim set up through his bad temper. Your quick-change artist did his act well. He hasn't told us where, but it was probably below the steps, that coat on in a flash, the bag hidden for a few minutes until he got back. But you both made mistakes. He got rid of the coat, but he kept the bag. The lab boys found a tiny dot of blood in it that matches your husband's DNA. We haven't found the murder weapon yet, but give us time, we definitely will.

As for you, your big mistake was to believe what your husband thought about us. He was wrong. I'm an old fashioned plodder, just like I said, but I do my job. WPC Dawson, read Mrs Young her rights and charge her with the murder of her husband. Before you say anything, Mrs Young, you're entitled to the presence of a lawyer, but I want to take you downstairs first for a glimpse of the man who loves you. A pity you both can't be together. You're so right for each other. Cigarette?"

THE LISTENER

Believe me when I tell you this: there wasn't a man who met her, no matter what he was or who he was, who didn't fall under her spell. Nobody was safe from her charms, young or old, and that includes that old geek of a clergyman with the bald head and glasses who called to see her once. He must have been in his seventies.

Yes, they all fell for her, and I can understand that, for I'd been through it myself. Why did nobody tell me or at least warn me what to expect? My mother should have told me when I was younger, but she was too stupid, too busy complaining about the things she said I was doing wrong. Anyway, why would she have told me; wasn't she a woman too, probably no better. That's probably the reason my father ran off and left us.

No, as I was saying, they all fell for her. The difference, the big difference, the terrible difference, is that I was the one who married her, I was the one stupid enough to.........I'm sorry, I'm OK now, it's just that I can't think or talk about this without my head tightening up inside. You can see my fingernails, they're bitten away to nothing. That's why I have to wear this broad Elastoplast over my knuckles, to stop myself biting them. Can't help it.

By the way, you'll notice I don't use her name. I can't bring myself to speak her name. No, as I was saying, every man who met her, even for a few minutes, went away thinking he was something special, that she'd been giving out signals only to him. How could he know, after all, that the very next man along would get the same treatment, and the next, and the next, and so on. And you know how she did it? Simple. She listened to them. Listened to them, with the face of an angel and those lovely big dark eyes wide open. She listened to every word, even if it was from some moron fixing the boiler.

She'd make them tea and they'd talk and you could see how special she would make them feel. They probably weren't used to anybody listening to their stupid tradesman's chatter, let alone somebody so beautiful, so beautiful and friendly, as my wife. I'd find myself standing there like a tailor's dummy while she listened and nodded and agreed and sympathised with some total stranger, encouraging him in the process to regard me as an obstacle, a problem, somebody in the way, somebody there just to open his wallet and pay out. How many of them came back later when

I was away I never found out. I never could catch her at it.

You're wondering why I let all this go, why I didn't challenge her right away. Ah no, I fell for that one once, only once, I humiliated myself only once, and what did I get: that innocent, bewildered look, as if it was all happening in my mind. If I hadn't known better I would have been taken in by her. That's how good she was, the picture of perfect innocence. I should have kept what I knew to myself, on that occasion, but I was so mad that I lost control and struck out at her. I've never seen a bruise go black so quickly. How well she covered it up with her make-up. Oh, she was good at covering things up, all right. If anybody did notice the bruising she said she'd banged into an open door. You see how smart she was - she wouldn't confess what she'd got it for. Oh yes, that angel face could deceive like a devil.

From then on I watched, watched and waited, but she was too good at her trade. She never slipped up once. I checked all her phone calls – nothing. She must have got them to phone her, you see. And no matter how many times I came home, at all times of the day, all I could see was that same look of innocence and surprise.

There's something I should have mentioned earlier: just after we got married I asked a few people from work round to the house, but she lost me them too. They could see through her, the innocent act didn't work with them. They visited only once, and didn't come back. Her sly advances put them off, but I'm sure she kept trying them on. I was isolated.

Things couldn't go on like that, as you can imagine. Everything came to a head when an oaf in a boilersuit came to repair the dishwasher. In she came, smiling and offering him tea and wearing her hair up. Yes, wearing her hair up just to show off that pretty neck. That was one of her favourite come-ons, but in this case one too many. The lovely neck exposed like that made things easy for me. You should have seen the surprise, the real surprise, when, after he'd gone, she felt my hands round that neck and realised, too late, that I'd known all along what had been going on. You can see the nice justice in it...........

The annoying thing is how some of the people here are so slow to see it. I've told them over and over what I've just told you, but they don't seem to listen; you'd nearly think some of them felt I was to blame. Well, if people won't listen, that's their own look out.

By the way, there's talk that I'm going to be moved out of here soon and in with the others, so you mightn't find me in this particular room next Friday. A pity, I like it in here on my own. Some of the men walking about out there look a bit odd to me. Well, goodbye, thank you for calling. It's been good to talk to someone who's willing to listen. I'll see you next Friday. You won't forget the cigarettes, will you?

A THING OF BEAUTY

Charlie parked on the darker side of the street. He took a quick glance at himself in the driver's mirror, and a deep breath to calm his excitement. He was Mr Cool. He rang Ray, his fingers quick on the glowing numbers.

Charlie knew exactly what his brother would think as soon as he heard his voice: *What does the little loser want this time, what kinda trouble is he in now?* He pictured Ray in his office above the night club, the big leather chair, the row of TV screens spying on customers and staff alike, the red phone, the one he was now dialling, that nobody, absolutely nobody, was allowed to use or answer but Ray himself.

It rang twice, was lifted, but nothing was said. "Ray, it's me. Charlie." A dry laugh at the other end. " I've hit it, Ray, I've hit the big one." Another laugh. " Honest, Ray, I've hit the big one this time." All the cool was gone. "You won't be laughing when you see this one, Ray. This is the end of 'small time Charlie'. Get ready to be impressed."

"Where are you?"

"I'm out here in Hazeldene in a 'borrowed' car. Relieving some of the good people of a few of their worries."

The laugh again. "I didn't think you'd be giving them a talk on good citizenship. What's this big hit you've made, or am I stupid even to ask?"

"You'll look stupid when you see what Mr Small Fry here has come up with. Have a bottle of champagne ready."

"OK, I'm a believer. What've you got?" Ray was familiar with Charlie's big scores that ended up hard luck stories, but there was something in his brother's tone this time that caught his interest.

"Ray, Ray, wait till you see it. It's right here in my breast pocket, close to my heart. You've never seen anything like it, Ray, I promise you. That's all I'm sayin', it's gonna be a surprise. I'll see you in about an hour. There's another one here I'm gonna do. I'm on a high, Ray, I'm on a roll."

And that's how he felt, that he couldn't put a foot wrong. First it had been the car. He was scouting for one when the man had pulled up and gone straight into an office with an armful of papers. He'd left the car unlocked, the keys in the ignition, and the seat warm for Charlie.

Then the big one, the stroke of luck that would win him real 'cred' from Ray and his crew. He had chosen fashionable Hazeldene at random, but again it seemed the gods were guiding him. As he cruised down the smart avenue he was just in time to see an elderly lady drive out between the pillars of one of the old detached houses. Charlie had driven past, turned, and parked a short distance away. He waited a few minutes. The avenue was deserted. The house was in darkness. Nobody answered his ring at the front door. In five minutes he was ransacking the bedrooms, the heavy velvet curtains closing in the lamplight.

The naivety of the public, especially the wealthy. Once the furniture was overturned, all those little private hiding places beneath were bare as a newborn baby.

He had collected a fair haul of jewellery and other valuables and was on the point of moving downstairs when he caught the big one. Something was wrong with the pair of slippers in the wardrobe, in the back corner. He got it. The other shoes and slippers on the wardrobe floor were pointed inwards, the natural position, but this pair had the toes facing outwards. Charlie checked. His fingers felt something hard in the toe of one of the slippers. He withdrew a piece of black velvet, unrolled it, and found himself with open mouth looking at the biggest cut diamond he had ever seen in his life, in book, on screen, or 'in the flesh'. It was an oval stone, beautifully faceted, and almost the size of a small egg.

Like most criminals of his type, Charlie knew the real thing when he saw it. He glanced involuntarily over his shoulder, realised he'd stopped breathing, and licked his dry lips.

His mind was instantly calculating what best to do with the rock, how to fence it, who would cut it. Three minutes later he was behind the wheel and half a mile away. What was that old boxing film Ray and he used to watch on video – *Somebody Up There Likes Me*. His laugh was more a giggle as he decided to phone Ray. He couldn't wait, he had to tell somebody. Ray always said that was why he would never make the big time, he hadn't the temperament for it.

Yes, the fates were definitely with him. He'd stopped at random to phone Ray and then realised he was in front of a house in total darkness. Half eight in the evening and nobody home; too late for people to be coming home from work, too early to be coming home from a night out. Charlie knew he should be getting out of Hazeldene in a hurry, but he was on a high, everything was opening up for him. It was too soon for the alarm to have been raised by the elderly lady. He parked a couple of streets away. He'd do this one quickly, as a kind of postscript. It wasn't greed, more a kind of buzz, an urge to keep the run going...

Julian Ablett was feeling more than a little precious. There was definitely flu on the way. He had gone to bed very early in the hope of sleeping off the symptoms, but had tossed and turned for over an hour and was farther from sleep than when he started. A phrase, or a line from a song, would pop into his head and go round and round without mercy. Julian wasn't even sure if he wanted to sleep. His dreams recently were very unsettling: brakes failing, feet bare, no clothes in crowded streets, hiding places uncovered by terrifying pursuers...

Then that feeling in his chest. It was more discomfort than pain, but should it, as Carol had insisted, be simply discounted as wind? Was he, in her words, becoming a 'real hypo', or was there indeed a tingling in his left arm, right down to the tips of the fingers. The pins and needles sensation seemed to be there every time he thought about it. Was this another penalty for allowing himself to get grossly overweight?

Such was Julian's mental and medical state when he heard the noise downstairs. At first he wasn't sure, but when he raised his head off the pillow and listened intently, there was no doubt. Somebody was moving about downstairs.

Whatever the condition of Julian's heart, it reached top speed now, right off the clock. Fear gripped him so hard it took his breath away, like he'd plunged into icy water. He briefly considered hiding in the big wardrobe, but he'd be sure to be found when the intruder did his rounds. If only Carol were there, instead of away at another one of those stupid weekend conference things. She would have known what best to do. Damn, he'd removed the bedside phone to prevent possible sleep interruption, and his mobile was downstairs. There was no option, he'd have to try to slip downstairs and out the back door, run across to the Watsons', and ring the police from there.

Yet Julian was afraid to leave the protection of the bed. He'd be so vulnerable, uncovered. Then he remembered Carol's weights and dumb-bells in the wardrobe. Strange, once his fingers were closed round the snug grip of the dumb-bell, he felt empowered, or at least a little bit the hunter, not totally the hunted. He eased himself through the half open bedroom door and started for the stairs.

Whoever was downstairs could now clearly be heard in one of the front rooms. As Julian tiptoed down, stair at a time, the thumping of his heart so loud he feared it would betray him, he suddenly felt an irrational impulse to laugh. All he needed was an old-fashioned nightshirt and nightcap and he'd be like the husband in one of those old Laurel and Hardy films.

That nervous fancy died in the same moment as three other things happened. He reached the bottom stair, the hall light was flicked on, and a man in dark clothes was staring at him from a distance of no more than ten feet.

The man instantly started towards him, without a word. Julian didn't intend it, it must have been a self-defence reflex action, but he closed his eyes and swung the dumb-bell in an arc towards the man. He heard a kind of dull crunch and at the same moment felt a shudder right up his arm and into his shoulder.

The sequence had lasted no more than seconds, but when it was over and Julian opened his eyes, the man was lying in a peculiarly twisted shape at his feet. There were no groans, no moans, just a trickle of blood running from the left ear. For a minute Julian was overtaken by an uncontrollable trembling, but he managed to steady himself and said, "Are you all right?" The question was so daft and his voice so shaky that Julian suddenly wanted to cry.

He didn't want to touch him, but he overcame his aversion and felt for a pulse. There was none. The man was dead. A terrible thought reached him. Had the housebreaker simply been making for the door, trying to get past him? Would this small man, half Julian's size, have been physically attacking him, or was it more likely that he was trying to get away from him?

It wasn't blind panic that seized Julian at that moment, it was terrifyingly clear-sighted panic. Police, court, trial, sentence, reprisal from the man's criminal cronies, career wrecked, marriage threatened, life ruined. He'd read and heard numerous stories of householders imprisoned for protecting their property, and even of successful personal injury claims made by the burglars. Now the headlines rushed at him: *Top Civil Servant on Murder Charge, Dumb-Bell Killer Gets Life*. Julian's hands were still trembling and a terrible nervous sickness was rising from his stomach into his throat. Then another fear hit him. Was there an accomplice waiting outside, an accomplice who would come looking when his mate didn't return? All the while he was trying to hope that this was one of his bad dreams...

Julian eased the Land Rover Discovery through the outer reaches of the city, dreading a police road check or some other unimagined danger. Amazingly, in there somehow with the overwhelming sense of fear and the terrible tension that was hammering in his head, was a tiny grain of excitement. Missing entirely from the mix of his feelings was any trace of guilt. Like most of his friends and colleagues, Julian feared and hated the criminal classes.

He could hardly believe that in person, by himself, he was doing these things, things seen only in films, things done always by other people. The body was now in the back of the vehicle, covered by a blanket and old newspapers, and he was on his way out to the old graveyard near the spot where Carol and he used to exercise Rudi.

Carol. How was she going to take the news that he had killed a man? There was a time he could have confided in his wife, sure of her support, but since the discovery that she couldn't have children she had changed. Now her career was all that mattered. Julian had been sidelined. He decided there and then, he wouldn't tell her, not until the dust had settled. There was no way of knowing how she would jump. It was better that she knew nothing. At least, not yet.

The decision not to call the police but to dispose of the body had not been a difficult one, in fact it hadn't been a decision at all. There was no way he could let this thing become public. All right, some people, perhaps many, might have admired and supported him, but Julian Ablett would always be known as the man who had killed a burglar. How could he go through the rest of his life with that reputation? No, the only decision had been how and where to get rid of the body, and his desperation had prompted the answer: put it where dead bodies usually go, into a graveyard.

He was wearing old dark clothes, the same uniform as the dead man was wearing. The point wasn't lost on Julian; embarked on a course of criminal behaviour, he was already dressing as a criminal.

In the back of the Discovery, packed round the body, were his gardening spade, shovel and small wheelbarrow, together with two large plastic bags. The evening was dry and visibility good, one of those September evenings when it never becomes totally dark. His mind raced ahead. Would the old road be closed off, or would there be a courting couple parked in view of the graveyard entrance?

As Julian dragged the corpse out of the vehicle and let it droop into the barrow, the head turned and for a horrible moment an open eye was looking up at him. Julian shuddered. He did so again when his hand touched the cold mushroom flesh of the face, but he managed to cram the body into the box of the barrow and spread the limbs as evenly as he could to prevent the load tipping sideways as he wheeled it towards the graveyard.

The place was even more desolate and overgrown than he had remembered it. Julian wondered if all the families represented by the tilted and broken gravestones had died out or moved on, or if some lingerers still arrived dutifully on set days with memorial flowers. It was hard to imagine bright flowers in this place of grayness and decay.

He chose a path that seemed negotiable and wrestled the wheelbarrow with its terrible cargo over grayish moss, through brambles and long spiky grass, to a forsaken corner, close to an ancient yew. Julian raised one handle of the barrow and the body tumbled out. He quickly returned to the vehicle for the tools and plastic bags.

One of the first outdoor alterations Carol and he had made when they had bought the house was to have the old flagging at the back lifted and replaced with a rectangular lawn. Julian had watched the workmen prepare the ground and place the squares of new turf, patting them flat with the back of their spades. It had been costly but quick, they had a mature lawn in less than a week.

His plan was to do the same, to cut out a body size area of square turfs, dig out a hole and stuff in the body, smooth it over, replace the turfs and pat them into place, wheel the surplus soil in the plastic bags to some other part of the graveyard, and either scatter or dump it well away from the burial place.

It wasn't that easy in practice. The roots of the old tree had spread everywhere, making digging difficult and cleanly cut turfs impossible, especially when the straggly grass preferred to break into small clumps. Julian's arms ached, he hadn't worked so hard in years. Fortunately the burglar was of small build, and in about an hour he was 'laid to rest', the area fairly well reinstated, and the excess soil broadcast on the other side of the graveyard. During the whole operation Julian's nerves had been continuously on edge, waiting for the lights or sound of an approaching car. When he was finally behind the wheel, the sweat on his back was cold, his shirt was sticking to him, and he was quivering with nervous exhaustion.

He stopped half way home, dropped the muddy plastic bags into a builders' skip, and finished his evening's work by hosing clean the tools and wheelbarrow in the back garden. The crime dramas he liked on TV were his Operating Instructions. After a bath he lay down exhausted, and, incredibly, slept until ten next morning. Even before a cup of tea, he tied everything he had worn the previous evening into a black binbag, took it to the local Civic Amenity Centre, and dropped it in one of the skips.

The thought rambled into his mind that his heart must be in fair condition after all, to have held up without a murmur through the hell of the past twelve hours...

Did he suspect her? Did he know something about Stuart and her? From the moment Carol had come home from her 'conference' Julian had been acting strangely. He seemed wound up, on edge. A couple of times he had seemed on the verge of saying something, but had turned away in silence.

Yet how could he know anything? Stuart and she had been as careful on this occasion as on the others; they had used new names to book into the hotel, she had fabricated the usual conference agenda, arrived back with the familiar phoney conference literature, and complained just as usual about some of the tiresome speakers and shoddy presentations. There was no reason for him to be suspicious. If he had tried to get in touch with her it would have been on her mobile. Yet there was an undeniable tension between them, in the air, all around the house.

A neighbour rang the following evening for a gossip. "...And by the way, did you hear about Mrs Curtis being burgled? They took all her jewellery and small valuables. Friday evening, I think it was, when she was out at a concert or exhibition or something. Isn't she a friend of yours, Carol?"

She was, a recent friend, and a good one. They had met at the Dog Obedience classes. When Carol's Rudi was killed by a van, and Mrs Curtis's beloved Corey had to be put down the same week, they were united in grief. Carol decided to call with her on the way back from the gym. She mentioned it to Julian on her way out. He was immediately interested, more than interested, startled. That was unusual. Julian rarely took any interest in her friends. Yes, he was definitely behaving oddly...

Ray knew for sure now that something was wrong. Even if Charlie's big success story had collapsed, which wouldn't have been a surprise, he wouldn't have stayed away this long. No, he would have been in with some elaborate explanation, some unavoidable misfortune that was nobody's fault, or certainly not his.

What was it Charlie had said — *There's another one here I'm gonna do* — Ray would make a few enquiries. He'd start with somebody on his payroll at the local station, and move up to C.I.D. if he had to.

Jessica Curtis oozed breeding. Her house was old and untidy, some might even have said ramshackle. The furnishings looked sorry to have survived so long. Jessica's clothes betrayed a carefree ignorance of contemporary fashion, but she effortlessly embodied the cultivation that Carol, and probably half the neighbourhood, tried to purchase.

"What I'm going to tell you now, Carol, I've been keeping to myself for about fifty years. I don't know why I'm telling you, there's nothing you can do, but it's so upsetting that I have to tell somebody."

"Of course," said Carol, and instantly thought it a foolish thing to say, but she was taken aback by Jessica's earnestness of tone and manner. She had offered a few words of sympathy over the burglary and now, it seemed, was to be entrusted with some deep secret or confidence.

"It's all right, the police have found my 'goods', as they call them, and I've identified them. I've not had them returned as yet, some kind of evidence fuss, but there's no problem there. They found them in a car parked round in Whitholme Gardens, not far from you, apparently abandoned. The residents reported it."

She hesitated. Carol could hear a clock ticking somewhere, and faraway traffic from the main avenue. The tall old-fashioned standard lamp threw soft shadows across the couch, smoothing Jessica's face, highlighting her silver hair. She looked directly at Carol, her eyes gentle and sad, her expression wistful.

"There's something else. There was something missing, something they didn't find, or something they didn't include."

She stopped again, but Carol knew to keep silent, to wait.

"It's something that has been in my family for over a hundred years, handed down to my father, and then to me. I've had it since my father died thirty years ago." She sighed, and continued. "My great grandfather, you see, was British High Commissioner in India at the height of the Raj. As such, he had control of virtually all areas of government.

I've never been sure of the exact circumstances of how it happened, but the simple fact is, Carol, and you are the first person to be told this outside of the family, and even then there were only three or four..." she stopped for breath, "the simple fact is that my great grandfather stole a diamond, a diamond so big that it must be one of the most valuable cut stones in the world. He had seen both the Koh-I-Noor and the Orlov, two of India's most famous diamonds, and reckoned this was bigger."

Carol said nothing. Even if she had had something to say, she would have been too surprised to order the words.

Jessica paused again, as if best arranging the narrative. "As I said, I don't know the full details of the theft. All I know for sure is that the diamond belonged to the Maharajah of one of the Punjab States before they were united with the Punjab State itself. My father told me once that his grandfather had taken it on impulse and then wanted to return it, but was unable to do so because of the brouhaha the discovery of its loss had caused. That's all I know. My great grandfather was above suspicion, of course. It's believed that hostilities between two of the States shortly afterwards were over the disappearance of the diamond.

Anyhow, it was passed on to my grandfather and then to my father, who told me about it when I came of age, and left it to me when he died. My husband knew about it, of course, and wanted me to put it into a Safety Deposit Box or into a bank with some kind of safe storage facilities, here or overseas, but I somehow dreaded parting with it, letting it out of my possession. Silly really, I suppose. Might as well have been a lump of coal, for all the good it has been in a wardrobe for thirty years."

She stopped, dead years dulling the light in her eyes. Carol judged this pause an appropriate cue.

"How much is it worth?" she asked sympathetically.

Jessica gave a small, sad smile. "Carol, my dear, you can't put a price on a diamond like that. It's priceless."

"Thousands and thousands, I suppose."

Jessica smiled again. "You'd be talking in millions, not thousands, but you'd never be able to sell it, even if you wanted to."

"Could you not get it cut into smaller ones? That's what I would have done."

"No you wouldn't. Only a savage, a total barbarian, would do that to such a 'thing of beauty', and you're not that, Carol. No, its value for me has never been its worldly worth in pounds or dollars, but its unique, almost mystical beauty. I just couldn't bear to part with it."

"So where's the diamond now. Did the burglars take it with them and leave the rest in the car?"

"That's just it, I don't know. It was stolen with the others, but wasn't there when I identified my property. I couldn't ask the police about it, of course. I'm really worried, Carol. Either the thieves got away with it, or the police have somehow recognised it as stolen in the first place and are secretly investigating. There's another possibility. Maybe the police have kept it for themselves. Wouldn't that be rich, the diamond stolen for the second time by those supposed to be in authority..."

Julian met her at the door. He'd been drinking, a thing odd enough in itself, but his entire behaviour was strange. He paced into the kitchen and she heard him refilling his glass, then returned, started to say something, stopped, emptied his glass in one go, refilled it again in the kitchen, and was standing before her with a distracted look in his eyes.

Carol was genuinely alarmed. "Julian, what's wrong?" she asked. She expected a barrage of accusations. What she got was a confession to murder.

Julian told her everything in a voice that started as a quiver and soon became a sob. It was as if by telling her every detail he could involve not just her understanding and sympathy, but somehow also her responsibility.

"You can't believe what I've been through, Carol, you can't believe it. I've kept it to myself as long as I can, but when I saw you going to console that woman I could stand no more. I'm his victim too, Carol, he's robbed me of my peace of mind forever. I just know it was him I killed, the same man, but you have to believe me, it was pure accident. What would you have done? Tell me I've done the right thing. If only you'd been here...." The confession trailed off in a self-pitying whine.

"Did you search him before you buried him, Julian? I mean, he could have had some of our stuff in his pockets, and if he was ever found it might lead back to us."

"No, he had a small bag with a couple of our things from the front lounge, but I got them back and burned the bag."

Carol's relief was palpable. "Julian, there's something worrying me. OK, so you covered up well where he's buried, but that was at night and you were in a hurry. Maybe in daylight it would be a different matter. Somebody might be suspicious. We need to go back out there and check. It's the only thing that could give us away."

For the first time in years Julian Ablett took his wife in his arms and gave her a hug of real affection — *it's the only thing that could give us away...*

"Stuart, it's the answer to everything. He took me out and showed me where he buried the body. I know exactly where it is. That diamond's going to give us a new life, a new start, it'll set us free. All we need to do is go out there and half an hour later we'll be worth a fortune."

Stuart sipped his beer, the dark eyes that she loved thoughtful. "We'll do better than that, Carrie. We'll bury the body somewhere else. If your darling Julian ever tries to come after us, or make things difficult, it'll give us a little bit of protection." Larger blackmail ideas were starting to form in a mind that matched the eyes.

Ray, now D.C. Denning, accompanied by a minder, alias D.C. Henderson, was making door-to-door enquiries. He knew the lingo. He'd been on the receiving end of it often enough.

"We have reason to believe a serious crime was committed in this area last Friday evening, and we wondered if you could help us with our enquiries."

One phone call had bought him the information about the stolen car and its contents, found abandoned in the Hazeldene district. Ray knew at once it was Charlie's work. He always parked somewhere close to the job, but not too close.

They had done two streets. It wasn't as straightforward as Ray had hoped. Many of the big detached houses had been rented for private medical practices and solicitors' offices, but at least that narrowed the range.

As soon as the door was opened Ray knew he had hit gold. It was as though the man had been expecting them. Ray could almost smell his fear. He gave his usual doorstep spiel, and asked if they could come in just to go though some routine questions. As they were proceeding down the wide hallway, the man regretting that he could be of no help, Ray politely produced a gun, stuck it into the double chin, and advised, "You've got ten seconds to tell me what's happened to my brother, fat man, or your brains are going to be splattered all over your Axminster."

Julian felt his knees go weak and feared he was going to faint. The gun was hard and cold in his throat and the man's face was so close that it was out of focus. A voice that was his but must have been operating by independent means was saying, "All right, all right, please don't shoot, please, please."

They allowed him to sit, even brought him a drink of water. Julian was openly weeping as he pleaded his case. When it was over the smaller one, who hadn't said a word, remarked, "We can't do it here, Ray. Too many has seen us."

His partner gently stroked Julian's temple with the muzzle of his gun.

"What was Charlie wearin'?" he snapped. Julian described the dark clothes. No, he hadn't looked in the pockets, no, he hadn't checked the breast pockets of the jerkin.

"We'll check this out, Freddie. We owe it to him, the poor little sod."

However bad an experience may be, it can get worse. The first time Julian had driven out to the graveyard his company had been the corpse of a murdered man. The second time his wife had been with him to check out his handiwork in the body disposal business . Now he was being taken there in the company of two criminals who, he had no doubt, intended to kill him. What was that saying, *third time lucky*. His only hope was that if they found on the body whatever they were looking for, and they didn't seem to know what it was, they might be sufficiently appeased to let him live. It was a faint hope.

The graveyard was deserted. Although it was not yet dark, the two men seemed not at all concerned about the possibility of other people being present. He led them directly to the 'grave', the smaller man carrying his spade and shovel.

Carol had described his turf reinstatement as 'well done'. It certainly didn't look that now. The turfs seemed disturbed, sunken, not nearly so well blended. Perhaps dogs or foxes or something had been scraping at them. The subsidence puzzled him. There was a distinct dip in the ground where he had been at pains to leave it level. Surely a body couldn't decay that quickly? As the two men watched, he started digging...

It was the same neighbour who had reported Mrs Curtis's burglary to Carol who raised the alarm. All week she had been ringing to relay gossip about her fellow suburbanites, but no reply from either Carol or Julian. Had they sneaked off on a holiday in hope of repairing the marriage?

Nosiness finally took her to the front door where Julian's four-wheel drive was sitting. Carol's car was away. Nobody answered her ringings and knockings. Her increasing fear that something was wrong was confirmed when she found the side door unlocked. Inside she found a week's mail piled behind the front door. The woman was too nervous to look upstairs. She rang the police.

They were on Carol's trail with very little trouble. She hadn't bothered too much to cover it. Initial enquiries revealed an affair that, as affairs go, was a poorly guarded secret, except to the husband. Further investigation showed that Carol had closed her bank account, emptying it of its thirty three thousand pounds, and for good measure had added to the tally another fifty thousand from the couple's joint account.

Luxuriating in the massive bed of their five star hotel suite, and in no hurry to finalise plans for their future, Carol and Stuart were engaged in mock dispute.

"What," she laughed, "get it cut in Bombay! Are you serious? The thing came out of India and it's never going back there. No, Amsterdam's the place, my lovely."

"No chance. Amsterdam's full of bad women. I wouldn't feel safe. I've never met a bad woman before."

Carol giggled and punched him on the arm. She felt as snug as the diamond in its safety deposit box, and every bit as radiant.

At Reception in the lobby six floors below her the Manager was assisting two detectives who were asking questions about the couple booked into the Kimberley Suite.

"Reno! Come on, you dirty beast." Honestly, that dog, if there was dirt anywhere in range, he'd be in the middle of it. Funny, she hadn't noticed that mound before. Fresh earth. Badgers probably. Looked like a grave, almost. The woman smiled at her little fancy; clever badgers, to replicate a grave in the middle of a graveyard.........

PENALTY

The entire penalty episode was one of those out-of-himself things that had happened to Ken a couple of times before, not unlike sequences on the screen where sound becomes blurred and everything goes into slow motion. He watched the No. 9 place the ball on the spot and walk back a few paces with the footballer's slightly bow-legged cockiness. A distant whistle blew somewhere in his head. Ken knew he had to dive to his left, as though he had seen or done it before. There was no surprise to feel his outstretched left hand make contact with the ball. Then, like a diver coming up through the surface, he felt normality burst upon him. Jubilant teammates were leaping on his back, and as he collapsed under their weight, he dimly heard the whistle that put them into the final...

A pre-recorded *Thanks, but I'm driving* message would have been useful. It seemed that everyone wanted to buy Ken a drink after the match, but he confined himself to a single pint.

Once the congratulations had receded, Maurice finally got a word in. "Typical. I miss a sitter at one end and five minutes later you bring off the save of the season at the other. It's time you found a mate who's a winner like yourself instead of a loser, big time, like me."

Ken laughed. "Stop moanin'. Think how the guy who missed the penalty must be feelin'."

Suddenly Maurice was unusually serious. "Well done, Ken. I don't mean just the penalty save. You're my good mate, my best mate, my only mate, whether you're saving penalties or not. Are you ready for another pint?"

"No, honestly thanks, Maurice. Can't take the chance. A Sales Rep needs a driving licence."

"Yeah, you're right. Well, here's to you." His pint disappeared at an impossible rate...

They were about half way home, through a drizzle that had already started when they came out of the club. Neither had spoken for a time. The car reeked of muscle rub from their kit in the back seat.

"What?" Ken suddenly asked.

"What? What d'you mean 'What'?"

"What is it? You've been watchin' me since we left the ground. What's wrong with you? Have you taken a fancy to me or somethin'?"

Maurice pounced on the opening. "What's wrong with me? That's a good one. What's wrong with me, and you sittin' there like a man under a death sentence." He turned off the car radio. "And you were the same back there in the bar. Man of the Match, probably Player of the Year, and you looked as if you'd sold the game. And you're askin' what's wrong with me? What is it, Ken, what's botherin' you?"

Ken rubbed the windscreen with the back of his hand. "Nothin'."

"C'mon, Ken, this is Maurice your mate you're talkin' to. I'm not stupid, y'know. I know there's somethin' worryin' you. There's somethin' on your mind."

Ken looked ahead into the rainy road, his face confirming the allegation. Suddenly he wrenched the wheel and swung into the big empty Social Services Building car park. He parked right in the middle and switched off the ignition. "OK, I woulda told you anyway, so why not now?" Then he sat back in the seat and said nothing.

"This looks heavy," said Maurice. "Have you got AIDS or somethin'?"

Ken released a long intake of breath and turned so they were face to face. "Maurice, we've been good mates now since the day I joined the club, and that's nearly six months ago, so you know what I'm gonna tell you is the truth, that none of it's my fault, even though you're hearin' only my side of the story." He paused.

"Go on," urged Maurice, "what is it?"

"OK, here goes. It's Nicola. You know I like her and all that, she's a nice girl, but she's your girl and that's fine with me."

Maurice looked puzzled. "So what're you tryin' to say?"

Ken picked a piece of Blu-Tack off the dash and rolled it into a ball between finger and thumb.

"Remember last Tuesday the three of us were meetin' in The Half Moon and you were late? Well, I bought Nicola a drink while we were waitin' and next thing she, … she starts comin' on strong with me, real strong, out of the blue, all of a sudden. She said it was me she fancied, always had been, and she was only usin' you to see me. I didn't know what to do. There she is tellin' me all the things we could be doin' together if we left before you arrived."

Maurice listened in silence, watching Ken closely.

"It's the truth, Maurice, I swear. I gave her no encouragement, none at all, there was none of it my fault, but it's been worryin' me ever since. I got up to go and right then you came in. You must've noticed the atmosphere was a bit tense. That's why I went home as soon as you arrived, even though you were expectin' me to stay."

The drizzle had increased to a steady rain and for a moment or two its beating on the roof was the only sound in the car. Then Maurice gave an odd little laugh and said, "It's all right, Ken, I know all about it."

"What! She told you about it? I suppose she blamed me?"

Maurice repeated the little laugh. "No, she didn't need to tell me about it. I asked her to do it. She was followin' my script." He peeled a stick of chewing gum, bent it in two, and popped it in his mouth, while Ken sat waiting for the punch line.

None came. Ken tried a little laugh just the same. "Your script? I didn't know you were into comedy sketches, with me as the stooge."

"It's not a joke, Ken. As a matter of fact, it's deadly serious. I asked her to do it, we rehearsed it together. It was a test. I was testin' you."

"You were what?" Ken felt his voice rising.

"Testin' you. You remember a few weeks ago you found my wallet in the car with nearly a hundred quid in it? That was a test too. I knew you were a bit short of readies at the time. You passed that one too with flying colours."

A redness was creeping into Ken's neck and over his face but his tone was more confusion than anger. "Maurice, what the hell's goin' on here? What's all this testin' stuff? You're not serious about any of this?"

Maurice looked him straight in the eye. "Remember that time we slipped outa' the Indian restaurant without payin'? That was another test: I wanted to see if you'd take a chance, break the law."

The hope of a prank ending gone, Ken's anger burst out in the volley of threat and abuse that comes with betrayal of friendship. Maurice sat calmly through it, expecting it, prepared for it. "OK, Ken, but just let me tell you why, surely you want to know why. You don't think I'd do all that without a good reason, just to test your friendship? If you're still not happy when I tell you why, throw me out in the rain, and you can drive over me too, if you want."

Curiosity prevailed over rage. "You better make this good, Maurice. I don't like bein' made a fool of. I expect my friends to trust me."

The rain eased briefly at that moment as if to allow Maurice the stage. He wound down his window and spat out the gum. When he spoke it was with an earnestness that he had never shown before in their half year of friendship. "Ken, I need somebody I can really trust, trust with my life, and I'm not exaggeratin'. I'm gonna' tell you somethin', somethin' I've never told anybody else. You're the first because you're my mate and I know I can trust you all the way. You've proved it."

"OK, but there was no need for all the testin' stunts."

"Fair enough, sorry, but I had to be sure, completely sure." He hesitated. "Y'see,

Ken, a year ago I killed somebody, a girl I was shacked up with. No, no, it was an accident, a pure accident, but it looked bad, or it woulda' looked bad if I'd been found out."

Ken had tensed at the confession, but he asked in fairly even tones what had happened.

"Her name was Kathy, and she was a few years older than me. Long story short, I was workin' my ass off for my finals, tryin' to make up for three wasted years. Kathy couldn't, or wouldn't, understand how important it was for me. She wanted me out with her on the town every night, instead of sittin' in studyin'. We were havin' rows about it all the time. She started goin' out with a coupla' very dicey friends of hers, and comin' home late, drunk and aggressive, you know the score."

"Yeah, an everyday story of city folk."

Maurice massaged his temples for a minute, rubbed his eyes, and continued. "Well, that night she came in about half eleven and started up as usual, callin' me all the worst names she could think of. I ignored her and that made her worse. I had all my notes and work in a pile, all in order, and she grabbed them off the table and scattered them all over the room.

I lost my temper, first time ever, and slapped her once, just once, not even all that hard, just a slap, and the nightmare began. Y'know in the old crime films how the victim trips and falls backwards and always manages to hit his head on a convenient fireplace? Well, Kathy must have read the script, for that's exactly what happened, just like in the movies, except this was real and she was lyin' there on the floor, dead, with a kind of froth at the side of her mouth." He paused, squirming in horror at the recollection.

"Why didn't you just tell the police what happened? It was an accident, after all."

"I've asked myself that question every day since. Maybe I should have, no, I definitely should have, but at that moment all I could see were finals missed, a trial, imprisonment, my life ruined, all the things that are supposed to happen to other people. Maybe it was just panic, I don't know. My mind was in such a state for weeks after it that I never did sit my finals, so there was no advantage there."

"So what did you do?"

Maurice drew a series of circles and squares on the steamy windscreen, reluctant to recite the details.

"There's no way of tellin' you what I did, Ken, without comin' across as a bad bit of work; all I can say is I was really desperate." He stopped. "All right, here it is. I rolled her up in a big piece of polythene a carpet had come in, hired a van next day, and somehow got her into it that same night. Lookin' back now, I don't know how

I went through with it - it was like I was somebody else. You couldn't imagine, Ken, what it was like to find myself in that situation, doin' those things."

Ken helped him out. "It is hard to imagine. It must have been a nightmare. But what on earth did you do with the body?"

Maurice closed his eyes as he recalled his actions. "I took her out to an old abandoned quarry we used to play in as kids. I dumped her over the edge. She was small and slim or I never could have managed it. The place is all shut off and grown over."

He paused. "She's never been found. I reported her missin' next day after I had cleared everything up and got rid of a lot of her stuff to make it appear she had maybe been plannin' to move out. The police suspected me, of course. They questioned me over and over, upside down, inside out. There was one real nasty one, with flat eyes sort of half hooded. He was like that actor Peter Lorre from the old films, if you know him. Every time I looked up he was starin' right at me with a sneery smile on, as if he didn't even believe my name when I gave it.

Anyhow, they turned the flat inside out, took stuff away, even went through my bin, but they couldn't find anything. I knew they were watchin' me, followin' me. I was gettin' paranoiac, thinkin' the flat was bugged, the phone was tapped, and never knowin' when the doorbell would ring and they'd be there to start the same questions all over again. At last, with no body and no evidence, they gave up, and I moved here a year ago to get away from the whole thing."

Ken sat in silence for a few moments, weighing up what he'd just heard. "It's a terrible story, Maurice, but how do I come into it? What's all this got to do with me?"

He'd hardly finished the question when Maurice was speaking, like a barrister who has spent necessary time constructing his case and has now reached the critical height of the argument. "Because I need you, Ken, need your help, and I know I can depend on it. Y'see, next year they're goin' to turn that whole area into some kinda' fun park or recreation centre or something. I happened to read about it. They're sure to find the body in the quarry and the whole thing will start up all over again. They'll open a murder enquiry, that's a cert. I couldn't go through all that a second time. No, I have to move it, Ken, but it's definitely a two-man job. Don't worry about what happens then, I've it all sorted, but the quarry bit is where I need you. You'll be 'aiding and abetting', all that kinda' shit, but I know you'll not let me down, that I can trust my best mate..."

The road was little better than a track, with long straggly whitish grass on either side, and clusters of rushes trespassing most of the way. They sat in silence, Maurice at the wheel of the Transit van, his mind on the job ahead. Both men were in dark clothes. Everything needed for the work was in the back of the van. The weather was in their favour, murky and, most importantly, dry.

The quarry workings had stopped in the 1940's and nature had very quickly reclaimed possession. Access to the quarry from below was now virtually impossible, so dense was the scrub. The road curved round in a spiral near the top of the quarry opening.

"A kid fell down it while I was still at high school," remarked Maurice, as he wriggled the van through a gauntlet of scratching whin bushes. "Broke his neck. They closed the whole place off after that. A few of us used to get in just to prove we could, but the place was soggy and dirty and we soon gave up on it. I'd say the only way in now is from the top."

"Wonder what sort of condition the body'll be in," said Ken, cutting across the commentary. "Will there be just a skeleton?"

Maurice kept his legs straight and his boots pressed hard against the rock face as Ken fed him down. His torchlight showed the rock wall smeared with green and dotted with gray and yellow growths.

"OK, steady, steady," he called up to Ken. It was odd to be sending up his instructions in a kind of very loud stage whisper; although they were miles from anyone, Maurice felt constrained not to shout up at normal volume.

The rope was tight and strong and good, and his boot soles gripped sure. He remembered the abseiling classes at summer school; incredibly, in spite of where he was and what lay ahead, Maurice felt a kind of athlete's satisfaction in his own competence and fitness for the descent...

"Ken, that'll do, I'm down," and, forty feet above, the dark figure outlined against the charcoal sky straightened and disappeared. Maurice's fear had been that, for whatever reason, the body would be missing, or impossible to find, or pulled apart by foxes or other scavengers. He could hardly believe it when his torchlight's very first scan caught the dull gray gleam of polythene. The body, like a large crudely wrapped package, was snagged in a broad bush growing at an angle from a bank at the base of the drop.

He could see the tape and the blue nylon cord. What a good job he'd made in trussing the little bitch up. How strong he had felt squeezing her scrawny neck until her feeble wrigglings and flappings had stopped. The slyness of her, searching through his things until she found the precious packet that represented his livelihood for at least six months.

So this is how you've been looking for work every day? So this is why you dropped out. You bastard. I know now where your money's been coming from. You're supplying freshers with their weekend party bags, their little packets of fun. You're the lowest form of life.

What did he care about her screechings, her hysteria? He started caring when she threw the priceless pack of white powder on the open coal fire; he cared enough to give a sob of rage and squeeze the pathetic life out of her ......

It was hard work dislodging the crumpled bundle from the bush, but no harder than he'd supposed. As he struggled to secure the rope round the slimy polythene a fold split open and something tangled in his hair. The wrinkled, rotten flesh, greenish black, had once been an arm.

Maurice pulled himself the last few feet to the top. The night was cool but sweat dripped freely from his hair and face. He threw himself down, exhausted but triumphant. It had actually been simpler than he could have hoped for: Ken had pulled the body up without too much trouble, and, when the rope had come back down, Maurice had simply done the descent in reverse. Perfect.

"We did it, Ken, we did it. Not easy, but we did it," he panted.

As Maurice raised his tired head he became aware of several dim shapes standing in a half circle in the darkness. He looked up to his mate for an answer. It came: "Maurice David Creelman, I am Detective Constable Kenneth Banks of Merton CID and I am arresting you in connection with the death of Katherine Aileen Magowan on May 22nd, 1999. I have to inform you that........."

INNOCENT

The phone sat on his desk, a bomb awaiting detonation. Drew licked his dry lips and took another deep breath. Snatches of conversation drifted across from the other end of the office - "sideways move, three more days' leave due" - the usual chatter that filled the day. Just talk, just words. Words. What were they after all, just sounds. And yet the power they had to make or break: *I love you; I'm leaving you.* Simple sounds, but able to save or utterly destroy lives.

He was doing it again, allowing, no, encouraging his mind to wander from the job in hand. And what was so difficult about the job? He was merely phoning someone he knew for a piece of advice, the sort of thing people do every day. That's what friends are for. Why the hesitation, then? Was it because since he'd got married he hadn't been in touch with Marty at all, not once? Drew recalled a remark his sister had made once when he'd rung her to borrow her stepladder - *The only time I ever hear from you is when you're looking for something.* But no, that wasn't the difficulty. If only it were.

Suddenly he reached out, lifted the receiver, paused for a millisecond, and dialled Marty's number. He listened to the ringing with his eyes closed, half hoping for no reply, but then Marty's familiar 'Yip?' sounded and the game was under way. Drew could hear the doowop his friend adored playing in the background; some things didn't change.

"Hello.... Marty.... This is Drew."

There was a pause. "Drew. I don't believe it. I thought you had died or emigrated or something."

Drew ignored the stab. "No, no, nothing like that. You know how it is, time just slips in."

Another pause. Marty ended it. "So how's married life treating you?"

Drew stalled. It was too soon. "OK, OK. How are things with you?"

"Not bad. I'm still looking for a job, or a job's still looking for me. I hear you're doing all right."

"Yeah, I suppose so - more work for the same money." They were still sparring, still circling each other. Drew decided it was his place to give ground. "It's nice hearing your 'oldies but goodies' still going there. They bring back a few memories.

You miss these things when you get married…. I suppose it's my fault, I should have kept in touch, at least given you a call to see how things were going."

"No problem, Drew, don't worry about it. I'll let you off this time with a yellow card."

A thaw could be heard in Marty's voice. Drew was sufficiently encouraged to narrow the focus. "I'm ringing you about something else, Marty. There's something I want to talk to you about, something I need advice about."

Marty gave a little self-deprecating laugh. "You're wanting advice from me. Have you got this the right way round, Drew? Since when has anybody ever asked me for advice? They ask me down at the bookie's what horse I'm backing, but it's only to make sure they're backing something else."

"It's a private thing, Marty. I couldn't think of anybody else I could ask."

"Thanks very much, I'm honoured - the bottom of the barrel, the Last Chance Saloon. It's OK, Drew, I'm kidding. Sure, if you think I can help, I will. Go ahead, what's the problem?"

"I'd rather not talk about it on the phone. Look, how are you fixed this afternoon? I could get away for half an hour or so."

Marty scanned ahead. "OK, not a problem. It'll keep me away from backing losers. What about The Central, like it used to be? About half three?"

"Fine. Appreciate this, Marty. Really do."

"Don't mention it…you're buying."

The Central was exactly the same as it had always been, right down to the crumpled customer at the end of the bar watching horseracing on the over-colourised TV. Drew had always thought of it as a dirty pub, but every time he'd checked it out there was nothing dirty to be seen. He'd finally put the impression down to the dark green interior walls and the low lighting.

"I still sink the black," came Marty's voice from the little recess, with its battered formica topped table and hardwood chairs. The sad-faced owner of The Central referred to it as the snug, which had always amused them. Drew waved over, got a gin and tonic, and waited while the barman scooped head after head off the pint of Guinness and retopped it, to no apparent advantage.

"Cheers." Marty made himself a moustache from the final topping and sighed his satisfaction. "It's never going to be Wine Bar of the Year, but you can't beat the old Central for a pint. Good seeing you again, Drew. So what's all this about?"

Drew sat silent, like an actor who has rehearsed his lines to perfection and dried up on the night.

"C'mon, Drew. This is your idea. I'm surely not 'only here for the beer'."

"No, it's just…it's a bit awkward. I'm not even sure if there's anything to it or not. Maybe I'm just imagining things."

"What? Have you seen Elvis, or is the man next door an alien or something?" Drew studied his drink, added another hint of tonic, and said, "It's Jane. It's Jane and me."

Marty spluttered a laugh through his Guinness. "And I'm the Marriage Guidance Counsellor." When he saw his friend's face, however, he abruptly pulled back. "Sorry, Drew. What's the problem?"

"I think maybe there's something going on, somebody else or something, I don't know."

Marty pulled his chair in close and wiped his mouth with the back of his hand. "Jane and you? No, Drew, no, I couldn't believe that. I mean, what makes you think there's something going on?"

"I'm not sure, it's nothing definite, just a lot of wee things."

"Like what?"

It was a relief just to be able to tell somebody, to release the worries that had tormented him since his suspicions began. Drew selected a few of the riper ones. They tumbled out.

"Well, I've noticed the smell of cigarettes off her; she doesn't smoke or allow smoking in the house, and yet she says she hasn't been out and nobody's been in. As well as that, I've rung her a few times from work and there's been no answer, but she tells me she's been in the house all day. It seems to happen just in the afternoons. Another thing, she told me last Thursday she really enjoyed an old Doris Day film on TV that afternoon, but I happened to find out at the weekend that it hadn't been shown, that the programme had been changed."

Marty swilled a mouthful of drink thoughtfully round in his mouth. "She's been having a wee smoke on the sly, or some of her mates are coming round for a puff. Maybe she's out shopping and doesn't want you to know how much she's spending, or she could be meeting her mates in town for a wee drink now and again. Women like having these wee secrets."

Drew scraped the label off his tonic bottle. "No, there's more to it than that. Something's going on, I just know it. I keep catching her out in wee lies."

"Well, have you pulled her about any of this?" Marty suspended the rolling of his cigarette for the reply.

"No, no, I haven't. There's nothing strong enough, nothing really definite. I'd probably just cause a big blow-up over nothing."

Marty finished the roll-up with mannish ease and lit it. "If it was me, I'd challenge her just the same."

"I know, Marty, I know you would, but that's not me."

"OK, then, tell me this. Has she been extra nice to you since all this started, nicer than usual, attentive and all that?"

Drew juggled the question until he caught the drift of it. "Yeah, yeah, I would say she has been, yes, she definitely has been. She's bought me a new shirt and a pair of driving gloves. Oh, and she's let me off doing the dishes a couple of times as well."

Marty's face darkened. "Don't like the sound of that, Drew, to be straight with you. Do you remember Betty Miller running out on Harry? Well, that's the sort of thing she was doing, being really nice to him and seeing some other guy behind his back . It really broke big Harry up when he found out. No, I don't like that, it's not a good sign."

Drew nodded with a perverse kind of satisfaction, as though he had expected such a result, was vindicated by it. In the poor light of the 'snug' his face looked gray. Marty was speaking again. "I'm not sure what more I can say, Drew. I still think you should have it out with her, tackle her straight on."

There was a long pause. Drew stared into his drink. Marty was finishing his, wondering if the 'meeting' was over, when Drew looked up and opened round two.

"Marty, to tell you the truth, it's more than advice I'm looking from you. I need a favour. I've no right to ask you this, I know that, but, the way things are at work, I can do nothing myself. You see, if I did ask Jane straight out, and there was something going on, she'd just deny it. I need proof, Marty. Now, please hear me out: would you, or could you, and I'd pay you for your time, keep an eye on her for me for a few days, just for a few days, and see if there is anything happening. See if she goes out, where she goes, if she's meeting anybody, or whatever."

"Nice one, Drew. What's the phrase, a hidden agenda? You've worked it well, but I'm not getting involved in this, Drew, it's between you and Jane, it's none of my business. You're asking me to spy on your own wife. It's not on, it's not on." Marty got up from the table. "You're forgetting Jane's my friend too, same as you are. You may ask somebody else, Drew, it's not my bag."

All the arguments Drew had rehearsed in advance paid off now. He pulled them out: only a real friend would be approached about a matter like this; Jane would never know Marty had been approached; he had the free time; the money would be useful; Drew would do it for him were their situations reversed...........

They arranged to meet again as soon as Marty had something to report. Drew got the call late Thursday afternoon and an immediate chill hit him in the stomach as soon as he heard Marty's voice. All Marty would say was that there had been 'a development' and they should see each other in The Central whenever it suited Drew.

The bar was busier than before, people having a quick drink after work, and the snug was occupied, but Marty was already there and had got a table behind the redundant jukebox. The place seemed even drabber than usual to Drew, and, in the mood he was in, he took this as a portent of bad news.

Marty was already making progress through a pint of Guinness. "I'll put this on your account," he explained, and Drew nodded his agreement. He didn't bother with a drink for himself.

The report Marty gave was inconclusive but alarming. He had parked in sight of the house after lunch on Tuesday and Wednesday and had seen Jane on each occasion, once putting stuff into the bin, and on the second day leaving out milk bottles. The whole business was seriously boring and he was about to give up on it about two o'clock that third afternoon when a taxi came down the avenue and stopped outside the house. Next thing Jane came out the side door carrying a blue sports bag and went off in the taxi towards the city centre. Marty had followed and watched her get out in Deacon Street. He was able to see her cut across the car park and go into the Melville Hotel on the corner of Reilly Place. By the time he had found a parking space and gone into the hotel lobby there was no sign of her.

"The guy on the desk is a wee weasel with a nose on him like the hood of a cooker. He said he hadn't seen anybody, it wasn't his business to see people, just to check them in and check them out. I had to give him a tenner to help him see. Sorry, Drew, it's going on your account, but it had to be done. Well, he suddenly starts seeing, says she arrives every Tuesday and Thursday and goes up to the second floor and that's all he knows.

'What sort of a hotel's this?' I asked him. 'People just walk in off the street and go upstairs and nobody asks them where they're going or what they're doing?' It was no use, he'd stopped seeing again. He's confident she'll be there next Tuesday, at least we've got that to go on."

Drew sat in unblinking silence through the report until it was finished. Marty had waited outside and about an hour later Jane had come out, still carrying the bag, still by herself. He saw her take another taxi and had to assume she was returning home, because by the time he'd got back to his car she was long gone. The close of the report was that Marty was forced to add his parking fees to the account.

Drew seemed to have got physically smaller. He had shrunk back during the hotel sequence, and now sat in abject helplessness, seeing nothing but his own ruin. He took the cigarette Marty rolled for him, forgetting he hadn't smoked in years.

"What am I going to do, Marty, what am I going to do?"

"Hold on, hold on, it doesn't look too good, I agree, but you needn't think the worst yet. There's only one thing to do. Say nothing to Jane, don't let her think you suspect anything, and next Tuesday we'll be back at that hotel. If anything's going on, we'll catch her in the act."

"Next Tuesday. How am I going to get through this, how am I going to get through the weekend?"

"You've no choice, Drew, you have to get through it. She's your wife, your whole marriage could be at stake here."

Marty took control. He got his friend a whiskey from the bar, punched him in the arm, and plotted out the course of action for the following Tuesday afternoon. Drew sat hunched at the table, only half listening, glad that somebody else was in charge.

The Café Montmartre across the small square gave them full view of the hotel entrance on the opposite corner. Drew had taken a half-day and they had eaten lunch in the café, or at least Marty had eaten his. Drew was too sick in the stomach to take anything other than several cups of black coffee.

"I'm hoping she doesn't show, Marty, and I'm hoping she does; I have to find out what she's doing, just to get this settled one way or the other." He checked his watch for about the twentieth time. " It's half two, she would have been here before..."
Marty's nudge stopped his mouth talking and started his heart thumping. There was Jane, there was his wife, striding over to the glass doors of the hotel, carrying the blue bag exactly as Marty had said.

"Come on, Drew, show time, let's go."

"I can't, Marty, I can't. My legs have gone weak. I swear, my legs have gone weak. What am I going to do?"
Marty's grip, and his voice, were rough. "Don't start any nonsense, or I'll leave you to sort this out by yourself. Come on, she's your wife, not mine. Pull yourself together."

The hotel lobby was empty apart from a few elderly guests resting and reading newspapers in its deep armchairs. Marty placed Drew behind a large artificial palm.

"You stay here and I'll check if the weasel has found out anything. He's maybe been seeing a bit more in the hope of another piece of paper in his hand."

Drew felt sick. There he was, watching his friend talking across the desk to a hotel clerk, and the subject of their conversation was his wife. It was like a scene from some sleazy film.

Marty came back shaking his head. "No joy. All he knows for sure is that the lift stopped as usual at the second floor. He wouldn't tell me which rooms are occupied, so we'll have to find out for ourselves."

There was graffiti and a crude drawing on the walls of the lift. They depressed Drew even further. The corridor on the second floor seemed to stretch forever. It smelt of used bedclothes.

"How are we going to find her in a place this size? Even if we get the right door, she might not answer it."

"Well, have you any better ideas?" Marty was losing patience with his friend's helplessness.

It was as hopeless as Drew had feared. The first two rooms produced no reply at all; the third one was occupied by a little frizzy-haired man in a yellow waistcoat. He made no reply to Marty's 'Sorry, wrong room' and watched them suspiciously for a few moments before closing his door. They pushed through a pair of fire doors into the kind of deep thumping music usually heard pulsing from boy racers' car windows. It came from a room with a narrow squared-glass panel in the door.

"Take a look at this lot," Marty invited Drew as he peered through the glass. "The things you see when you haven't got your camera."

Drew mechanically obeyed. He was looking into a large conference or function room. About thirty women, all ages and all sizes, dressed in a variety of exercise gear from leotards to track suits, were heroically keeping pace with a Jane Fonda wannabe who was finding enough breath between stretches, bends and jumps to yell out random calls of encouragement to her disciples.

Drew had just straightened up from the peepshow and rejoined Marty to continue the search when his mouth literally dropped open in surprise. Through the double doors, in full aerobics kit and with a towel round her neck, strolled Jane. Her surprise on seeing Drew was even greater than his own.

"Drew! What on earth are you doing here?"

He would never have believed Jane capable of such rage. It terrified him. She banged the blue bag down on the kitchen table, her eyes blazing.

"I just can't believe this. I don't believe it. I'm never going to forgive you, Drew. And you actually hired that layabout to follow me! How do you think that makes me look? How do you think it makes me feel? He'll have a great laugh about this with his mates down at the bookies. I'll never think the same of you again, Drew."

Drew winced with guilt and shame. "I know, Jane, I know. You don't know how sorry I am. If only you'd told me earlier I'd...."

"But that was the whole point." She ripped a sports shoe out of the bag with such fury that he thought she intended throwing it at him; he half hoped she would, to satisfy part of her anger. "Can you not see, that was the whole point? It was supposed to be a secret. This was going to be my secret for you, losing a few pounds for my bikini in Lanzarote. Now you've ruined everything. I'm not going on holiday now, you've spoiled the whole thing. And it was you who said you thought I was starting to put on weight. I was doing it for you, and you have me followed like a criminal. How could you think those things of me?" She hurled the empty bag into the corner, dumped the kit on the floor, and stormed into the lounge. Drew drooped after her.

"I'm sorry, Jane, I'm so sorry, you'll never know how sorry. I promise I'll make it up to you. It's just that I was so worried because I love you, Jane."

"Love me?" The bitterness in the words crushed him. "Love me? How can you love me when you don't even trust me? I know now what you really think of me."

"No, Jane, no, I'll never doubt you again. Please forgive me, it was all my stupid fault, my bad mind. I don't deserve it, but please forgive me. I love you, I really love you..."

"She loves me, Marty, she loves me, and that's the only thing that marrrs." Drew was drunk, he knew he was drunk; he didn't care, in fact, he must remember to get drunk more often. No, he didn't care about anything.

That was why, when Marty had presented his 'account', he had thrown in an extra couple of tenners. Now, as he was staggering home from The Central supported by his pal, his head felt light with gin and gratitude.

"Marty, Marty, my old mate Marty, where would I be without you? How can I repay you? You name it. Money means nothing to me now. I've a wife who loves me, and I've the best mate in the whole wide worrrllaaaagghh..."

Just in time Marty got out of the range of fire as Drew was copiously sick over the pavement.

She unzipped the blue bag. They were in his bedroom as usual.

"Well, how was he this morning?"

"He was up sick most of the night, but he's away into work full of apologies and Alka Seltzer."

Marty sniggered. "By the way, you really looked the part. I think I'll sign you up for that keep-fit class of my sister's."

She withdrew a pair of frilly black panties from the bag. "Don't bother. This kind of workout's good enough for me. And remember, no cigarette after it…"

COUNTER MEASURES

"Sixty."

There it was again - no 'Good Morning' or 'Please' or 'Thank You', not even a 'Sixty pence' or 'Sixty p'. Just 'Sixty' and the hand stretched out for payment before the newspaper was passed over the counter. Ronald tried once more not to be irritated; as a senior Civil Servant not far from retirement he should be able to ignore the bad manners of this little Pakistani newsagent whom he saw for only a few minutes on his way to work.

Yet the more he had tried to overlook the man's rudeness, the more clearly he had focused on it. For just over a month now he had been a member each morning of the short, quick queue in Patel's Newsagents buying their papers and sweets and cigarettes for the working day ahead. He had chosen Patel's quite at random when his regular newsagent had discontinued the early morning delivery service. There were two other shops and a newsstand on his route to work that could just as easily have supplied him with his Daily Mail: why, then, did he continue to use the one whose owner's abrupt manner got under his skin every weekday morning?

There was nothing at all racist in Ronald's feelings about the man's behaviour; he would have felt the same way had the newsagent been his own brother. No, it certainly wasn't that, but Ronald had found Patel's manners and mannerisms disagreeable right from the first morning - the man never looked at the customer he was serving but continually checked the doorway and street outside the window for further business; he seemed to have an aversion to physical contact and either set customers' change on the counter or dropped it into their hand; he displayed the papers behind the counter on sloping shelves, and handed them over only after payment had been made; there was never a greeting, just the flat announcement of the sum owed, accompanied by the open hand.

The first few mornings Ronald had offered the usual pleasantries, but the man had been almost offensive in his urgency to serve the next customer. At that busy time of morning the last thing Ronald Munro, or anyone else in a hurry to work, would have wanted was a chatty shopkeeper, and no doubt Patel's style suited his early customers, but Ronald nonetheless couldn't help taking exception to what he saw as an unacceptable absence of basic good manners.

Not that Ronald considered himself a critical or intolerant type, but he had always been alive to irritating personal habits and singularities in other people. His wife's, for example, derived from her overly gentle nature, but although he knew this, they annoyed him just the same - taps left dripping, doors not firmly closed, jars with lids unscrewed.

In her case he could speak his mind and get things seen to: less manageable were those individuals he had to meet on a daily or regular basis. Matthews at work, as an instance, drove him nearly spare with his endless tuneless whistling, and equally maddening was Finney, he of the limp handshake, who answered the phone a hundred times a day with his hilarious 'Hello, hello, hello' routine - Donald waited for it and cringed every time.

Now here was Patel, this ferrety little middle-aged man with the anxious brown face, Charlie Chaplin moustache, and ignorance of elementary politeness. Ronald made sure to touch the fingers, black with fresh newsprint, as he gave them the pound coin they wanted, and he did the same before his change could be dropped into his hand.

He was surprised to find the matter occupying his mind during the day. He couldn't share it with anyone, of course: a man of his seniority would have been privately laughed at for allowing such a petty thing to occupy his thoughts.

It was clear that Patel's behaviour comprised two main, interrelated elements, rudeness and greed. The first was a tricky one, perhaps involving different cultural practices and forms of trading; Ronald vaguely remembered pictures of eastern markets and hands stretched out in bazaar dealing rituals. Greed, however, was more universal, more personal, and certainly more open to attack. Ronald looked forward to his next visit to the little cluttered shop that smelt of curry and raw, early morning cigarette smoke...

"Sixty."

"Thank you," and Ronald released a jackpot of 1p and 2p coins into the open hand. Patel hesitated, the little dark eyes darting anxiously along the queue: should he assume the sum was correct and take the chance of being diddled, or should he waste time counting the coins, and risk losing an impatient customer at the back of the queue? He unhappily set down the handful of coins in a loose pile, no doubt to be checked later, placed the Mail on the counter, and was already serving the next customer before Ronald had time to pick it up. Not once during the transaction had Patel even glanced at the customer who had unloaded all that small change upon him.

The following morning Ronald employed a different tactic: "The Daily Mail, please, and some of those, wait a minute, what d'you call them, those little red fruit sweets, not bon-bons, is it pastilles or lozenges, can't be sure, but got them in this shop a few weeks ago, can't see them now, in a roll or a tube or something, or was it a box, can't remember, but it was yellow, definitely yellow, about 30p they were, soft centres, sugar coated, they're for my wife, I don't eat sweets, trying to cut down a bit, trying to lose a few pounds after the excesses of Christmas......."

Ronald would have stretched the performance a bit farther, so much was he enjoying the desperation in Patel's face, the frantic eyes, the twitching black moustache, but the natives in the queue behind him were decidedly restless, and he settled for a homely tube of Smarties. The triumph was clinched when on his way out of the shop he noticed a young man detach himself from the end of the line and dive through the door looking anxiously at his watch.

Over his coffee that morning Ronald reviewed his strategy with great satisfaction. He didn't hope for a minute to alter the man's behaviour significantly, or raise his manners to an acceptable level, but if he could be a spanner in the works sufficiently for Patel to have to acknowledge him, look him straight in the face, treat him as an individual customer, then he would consider the victory his. The possibilities and permutations of disruption before him seemed infinite...

And so it proved. "Could I have half a dozen of those balloons, please?" pointing to a box stuffed in between top shelf and ceiling. Then, once the stepladder had been dragged out and the box brought down and dusted off, "Now, I need one red, one green, one blue, one yellow, one orange and one white, please."

Another morning Ronald 'accidentally' dropped his pound just as the hand was about to claim it, and the resultant search among the feet of the other customers went on a minute or so longer than it needed to. Patel was itching to move on to the next in line, and by the time Ronald pressed the coin into his palm the little man was chewing his moustache in impatience.

If Ronald was enjoying his private little campaign, especially the devising of different delaying tactics each morning, he certainly couldn't claim much success for it. Not once did Patel look him directly in the face, or reveal any recognition that it was the same customer every morning who was causing him such inconvenience and anxiety. Any response there was to Ronald's daily nuisance games came from the queue behind him, ranging from expressions of impatience and irritation to outright threatening on one occasion. Ronald reassured himself that he was having an effect, however, because by the end of the first week of his crusade he was certain that business was down and the queue shorter in the little shop. Things would have to come to a head, Patel would have to react one way or another, and that in itself would be a flag of surrender...

The flu that laid Ronald Munro low for two weeks struck with merciless speed. He had gone to bed with a slight headache and woke next morning with a sharp stone stuck in his throat, a jagged stick in each ear, hammers battering his temples, pincers squeezing his arms and legs, and an icy shivering mocking his boiling face. Ronald normally struggled into work, no matter how he felt, brushing aside Mary's remonstrance, but on this occasion he was too unwell even to consider that course. His GP, who called next day, predicted "ten days at least" off work, identifying the strain as a particularly virulent one that he feared was making the rounds of the district.

Ronald was surprised how weak he was, how light-headed, as he set off on his first morning back. He thought of Patel's and smiled: he would wait a day or two to get his strength back before he resumed the offensive. At present it seemed unimportant, and maybe the little newsagent would see that he looked haggard and gray and honour him with a welcoming "Good Morning. Nice to see you back." Ronald smiled again, at his own ironic humour.

For a second or two he thought he had stopped at the wrong place, was looking at the wrong shop. What should have been Patel's Newsagent in old-fashioned hand painted style was now an illuminated Perspex box supplied by Pepsi Cola and bearing the bold letters **Mini Market**. An automatic door introduced Ronald to a blast of warm air. Along vinyl aisles of plastic racks people were choosing their sweets and papers and drinks, and carrying them to two little check-outs, watched over by a CCTV camera and fluorescent lighting. Ronald was amazed at the transformation of the shop itself, which had been enlarged, restructured, and stripped of any resemblance to its former appearance.

He recognised a regular from the Patel morning queue, his daily packet of cigarettes looking solitary and silly in the white shopping basket.

"What's happened here?" he asked him. "Where's Mr. Patel?"

"What's happened? I'll tell you what's happened. They were in here the day after he left, and had the whole place gutted. The whole place gutted. They had it the way you see it now in only a coupla days. A coupla days."

"But what about Mr. Patel? Where's he?"

"Patel? He's away back to Pakistan, or wherever he's from. His mother died, and he had the place sold the next day. The next day. Daft little sod – he was sendin' back every penny he made to keep her looked after in some kinda hospital. Never spent a penny on himself, they say. Never a penny. You knew him yourself, you could see he hated havin' to live here and run the business, hated it..."

Ronald's flu symptoms were gone, but over his morning coffee he couldn't focus his unblinking eyes on the Mail, couldn't concentrate on the black print in front of him.

INTEGRITY

Jerry loved the period immediately before Matriculation and Freshers' Week. Every university town had its crop of eager young students scrambling for accommodation, every advertising space was crammed with *TO RENT* notices, and every day was a fresh opportunity for him to harvest some of the newly arrived student grant money.

The ads in the shop window ranged from biro scribblings on Post-its to professionally printed Sales Cards. Jerry's eye instantly eliminated everything but the best quality notices. There were six of these, all of the same design and manufacture, advertising just two flats, three cards for each. The contact telephone number confirmed that both sets belonged to the same owner. Jerry settled for the one that read: *3 Bedroom Flat to Let   Fully Furnished   Close to University   Suitable For Young Professionals   No Students*

He made a note of the number and hurried back to the Volvo Estate. In the back were suitcases and large, tied cardboard boxes, all of them empty, and a couple of loose items - a pot plant, and a small globe of the world on a stand. He lit a cigarette, dialled the number and briskly arranged to meet the landlord, Mr Singh, outside the ground floor flat in Granada Avenue.

Noor Asan Singh loved the period immediately before Matriculation and Freshers' Week. Not that he had any liking for students. He regarded them as bad tenants, a tribe of people all too likely to devalue property in a district, if the market were not carefully controlled. No, their usefulness lay in creating for a short spell an artificially swollen demand that he could craftily exploit to inflate his rents more than was possible at any other time of year. Noor made certain that he always had flats available at this time of year, even if it meant one or two lying vacant for a month or so in advance. He had perfected the timing over his seventeen years in the business.

The Granada Avenue property. He liked that phone call. The man had been businesslike. Singh was experienced enough to recognise probable time wasters. He would be sure to have a squirt of breath freshener before they met. Some people were put off by garlic.

Jerry played it perfectly. He sensed the faintest hint of deference in Singh's handshake with this striped suit businessman carrying a pure leather briefcase.

"Dalzell," he announced. The name for many clearly meant boss, manager, sahib. Singh's eye took in the car and the cases, the man's perfectly laundered appearance. This was the kind of tenant he wanted. How high could he go without overbalancing the scales?

He showed Dalzell round the flat, pointing out its features and advantages, the recent improvements, the quality of its fittings and furnishings. Dalzell, unlike most chattering prospective tenants, said nothing at all, just sauntered behind, so that Singh couldn't be sure if his promotional tour was a hit or completely missing the target. He found himself repeating the same information to fill the gaps, and ended up almost apologising for a property he would otherwise have been celebrating.

When the whole flat had been comprehensively explored, including the glory hole and the outside bin bunker, Dalzell suddenly snapped, "Well?"

For a moment or two Singh was taken aback, as though some kind of accusation had been made, until he realised he was being asked for the rate. Feeling unusually hesitant, he went for broke. "A thousand pounds a month."

Dalzell abruptly turned and walked away from him. Singh thought he had aimed too high, but Dalzell produced a mobile phone and tapped in a number.

"Ronald. Hello. Everything OK there? Good. Look, I've found a place here will suit us fine. Yes, it's furnished. Not bad. Get your stuff together, and Clive and you get up here on Monday morning. I'll arrange with the chap here to get some kind of one-year lease organised. I'll ring you later with the address and directions. Bring the Stanhope Contract with you. I'd like another look at that."

Dalzell turned to Singh next, and gave him his orders. "My partners will be arriving on Monday. Before then, get the papers in order. We'll take this for a year. I'll want some of these things removed," vaguely indicating the furniture, "but that'll do later. Just leave the key in the meantime. Come back at noon on Monday." Echoes of the Raj ran briefly round a ground floor flat in Granada Avenue.

Singh hesitated. This was against all normal practice. What about the month's rent in advance? What about the insurance deposit? He half opened his mouth to mention them, but the man had already withdrawn papers from the briefcase and was making another phone call. For him further business concerning the flat was on Monday's agenda, and Singh was no longer in the room.

Jerry watched through the curtain as his 'landlord' left slightly shell-shocked. Singh stopped briefly at the Volvo to examine its contents. He went on his way looking reassured.

Jerry got to work immediately. He produced from the case a handful of Flat to Let cards and carefully printed the same notice on three of them: *3 Bedroom Fully Furnished Flat   University Area   Gas Central Heating   Secure Entry   Private Parking Students Welcome*   Below he added his mobile number.   As in all scams where a mobile phone was used, he'd get rid of it immediately afterwards. In ten minutes he had the notices posted in three shop advertising windows.

Amazingly, the call came inside half an hour. Jerry was now Eric Worthington. He made an appointment for the three students to visit the flat at 2 o'clock. Let them wait a little while. Good things shouldn't come too readily.

The flat was way beyond anything they'd seen to date. The stringy, sandy haired one looked worried, his two companions were open mouthed. Jerry noticed the 'private' glances they were exchanging as he showed them the flat, and especially when they heard the rent. He took them through to show the private parking area at the back, and collected some papers from the Volvo Estate. He had to rummage among the cases and boxes.

"I'm off to London this evening, so if I don't find tenants before then, the flat'll have to lie empty for a year. Can you believe it, that damned family waited until yesterday morning before they told me they'd changed their mind about taking it. Left me in a right fix. People have no sense of decency at all." He delivered a brief rant on the absence of integrity in present day behaviour, concluding, "My father taught me to treat every man as a gentleman unless I found him to be a rascal. Nowadays it should be the other way round." They returned to the large living room.

"Now, boys, I'll need a quick decision. It's £750 a month, as I said. I'd require a month's rent down for insurance, repayable at the end of your lease, and a month's rent in advance."

They shuffled a bit, no one wanting to make a decision. "Could we have a think about it?" the stocky one asked. "We'd need to talk it over."

"Certainly. Rightly so. But not too long. I've three nurses coming to look at the flat at four."

The stringy one sipped at his pint mournfully. He looked up through lank hair that matched in colour the large freckle droppings on his white face.

"One and a half large. It's big money."

"It is and it isn't, Dessie." Tommy was sold on the flat. "Look, think about it this way. It's only fifty quid more each a month than that shithole in Cavanaugh Street. What were you getting there for your six hundred? This is a gift when you see all the things we'd be getting."

"He's right," seconded Don, the stocky one. "When he said 750 I couldn't believe it. I was expecting a grand at least."

"I know what's going to happen," resumed Tommy. "We'll wait until it's too late and end up taking some shitheap and blaming ourselves the rest of the year. This is a real chance. We're lucky to get it, dead lucky."

Dessie deliberated. "OK, but I'd like something back on my five hundred. Tell you what I'm gonna do. I'm gonna ring Addie and put him on to that car packed with all those cases. Addie'll have it away in a second while we're doing the business with Worthington. There'll be something in it for all of us."

His two pals chewed the idea over, but not for long. After all, once they had the lease signed and their money paid, what was the theft of Worthington's car to them. That would be his problem, nothing to do with his new tenants. They finished their pints to seal the agreement, before phoning Addie and going down to the bank to lift the readies.

The call couldn't have come at a better time for Addie. His gambling losses were getting him into deep, deep trouble. He had just had a visit from two of Gregson's heavies. Things were bad, dangerously bad. Gregson was putting serious pressure on for the two grand he owed him, and had given Addie only three more days. He took a deep breath. He just needed a break to get him out of this run of bad luck. Maybe this was it.

Addie despised Dessie and Tommy and Don. He had been at primary school with all of them and was smarter than the three of them put together. Now here they were offering him a job, but only to get a cut for themselves. Studying, degrees, education - bollocks. He'd outsmart the lot of them. He'd steal the car, all right, but not for their benefit. He'd ring Gregson and offer him the goods, get himself off the hook, get Gregson off his back. As for them, the smart university students - Addie laughed out loud - he'd tell them the boxes and cases were all empty.........

Jerry's shirt cuffs were white against the dark mahogany table as he passed over his gold fountain pen to the three young men to sign the fake tenancy papers. He was handing over the bogus receipt for fifteen hundred pounds at exactly the moment that Addie was driving his Volvo Estate out of the private car park. In the passenger seat sat the terrifying figure of Gregson's main 'enforcer,' who had been sent along to make sure this wasn't another of the little toe-rag's fairy tales.

Addie's hope was that the contents of the boxes would be valuable enough to clear his 'account' and get him back into Gregson's good books, with perhaps enough left over for him to back a few winners. He felt his luck was starting to turn.

The car cruised towards town, passing on its way the room in which Noor Asan Singh was minutely checking the one-year lease that three professional tenants would sign at noon on Monday. In Granada Avenue Eric Worthington handed the keys of the flat over and headed for the car that, fitted with new number plates, would take him to another university town..........

NOTES